ISLAND FICTION

LEGEND OF THE SWAN CHILDREN

Maureen Marks-Mendonca

Series Editor:
Joanne Gail Johnson

MACMILLAN
CARIBBEAN

DEDICATION

To my beloved brother, Francis

Macmillan Education
Between Towns Road, Oxford, OX4 3PP
A division of Macmillan Publishers Limited
Companies and representatives throughout the world

www.macmillan-caribbean.com

ISBN: 978-1-4050-9901-1

Typeset by Expo Holdings, Malaysia
Design by John Barker
Cover design and illustration by Oliver Burston

Printed and bound in China

2012 2011   2010   2009 2008
10 9 8 7 6 5 4 3 2 1

TIA LUCIA VANISHES

IT WAS TIA LUCIA WHO STUMBLED UPON THE BODY beneath the sprawling tree in the centre of the courtyard. Right away, she summoned the coroner, who also happened to be the only doctor for miles around. He came as he was, in pyjamas and rubber boots, his stethoscope sticking out of a pocket. After a quick examination of the old woman's twisted form, he looked at the angle of her cane on the ground, spied a cluster of juicy fruit just out of reach, and scribbled in his notebook before departing:

> NAME: Señora Lagrima
> TIME OF DEATH: Approx. 5:30 a.m.
> CAUSE: Heart attack while reaching with her cane for a mango.

But no one was buying that. The scent of intrigue was in the air. Amidst the fruit-laden groves in the courtyard, down the squeaky corridors of the great house, and in the shade of the cocoa and coconut trees across the road, whispers abounded. What about the strange symbol squiggled in the rust-coloured dirt beside her cane? And who stole her star-gazing paraphernalia?

3

The following day, Alejandro was roused from an uneasy sleep by the voice of a stranger.

"Does he know?" a man murmured.

"I don't think so. His power is growing, but there is still a lot that escapes him," a woman whispered back.

Alejandro sat bolt upright. That was his mother's voice, and she was talking about him. He scrambled to the window alongside his bed and poked his head out. There she was standing barefooted among her herbs in the front garden, but the person she was speaking to was out of sight. A gust of wind blew her dishevelled hair away from her face, and Alejandro saw that she was gnawing at her lower lip. His stomach tightened.

"… strike soon," the man was saying, *"especially with Señora Lagrima gone."* He dropped his voice even lower, so that Alejandro could only catch snippets. *"… others … disappearing … no choice, Moon Woman …"*

Everyone else called Alejandro's mother 'Tia Lucia', because Lucia Vega Van Sertima was a healer. She cured the troubled young with her words of wisdom and eased the aches of the aged with her fragrant herbs. Few people knew her clan name.

Tia Lucia leaned forward, arms akimbo. She was petite, but fiery. *"¿Quién es? Who is behind this? Tell me and I will— "*

"Careful, Moon Woman, anger clouds the heart and tricks the mind," the man warned, raising his voice a tad. His strong arm, a darker honey colour than Tia Lucia's, reached out and pressed something into her hand. *"Just leave it to me, I will find out soon enough. Go, and wait for my call."*

Tia Lucia passed a hand over her eyes with a deep sigh. *"Okay, my friend."*

Alejandro heard the shuffle of feet on the gravel walkway. The man was leaving.

"Remember to … and if … the panman …" His voice faded.

Alejandro charged down the passageway to the living room. He stuck his head out the front window just in time to see a flash of colour as the man disappeared around the side of the great house some distance away. He gaped in amazement. Their little wooden cottage was at the back of the estate, at the very end of the path that wound through the groves of mango, genip, and sapodilla trees. No one could move that swiftly.

"Buenos dias, sleepyhead," said Tia Lucia, coming towards the cottage with a smile that barely hid the strain in her eyes. "Looking for me?"

"Who were you talking to, Mami?" His hair hung thick and wild about his face, falling into his eager oval eyes and exposing his bat ears.

"A friend." Her eyes narrowed as she watched him keenly. "An old friend."

"What was he saying about the panman?"

With a sharp intake of breath, Tia Lucia's eyes darted through the window to a spot in the far corner of the living room, beyond his head. Alejandro turned too to look curiously at the exquisitely crafted silver figurine of a panman on top the woven wicker stand.

"Were you eavesdropping again?" Tia Lucia scolded, tweaking his ear.

5

"No," said Alejandro indignantly. "I could hear you from my bed, but I couldn't hear everything."

Startled, his mother blinked several times, then she chuckled. "You shouldn't have heard anything at all from the back of the house. Whispers are supposed to be private. To have a son with your ability is as much a trial as it is a blessing." She ruffled his hair.

"*¡Anda, Mami!*" said Alejandro, gripping the windowsill and rocking back and forth impatiently, "What did he say? *¡Di-me!*"

"He said be sure to keep the panman safe, okay my little Spanish inquisitor?"

Alejandro eyed his mother doubtfully. Her pretty moon-shaped face had a playful smile on it, but he knew something was troubling her deeply. "What's that in your hand?"

"Ahhh, this." Tia Lucia glanced at it briefly before slipping it in her skirt pocket. Alejandro caught a glimpse of something maroon and round. "Tomorrow, Alejandro *mi chiquito*, we are going to take a break from the sadness and go off on an adventure – just you and me. Go get showered and dressed. We have a lot to do today."

Alejandro did not move. He watched her walk back towards the garden, and when she was almost there, he said, just loud enough for her to hear, "Are we running away from the bad people?"

The skirt of her tan and brown dress swirled as she swung around sharply to stare at him. "Why do I try to keep things from you?" She made her way back.

"What do they want?" Alejandro was more curious than afraid.

Tia Lucia shrugged her shoulders helplessly. "I don't know, and until I find out, we are going to go someplace safe."

"When will we come back home?"

She reached out and touched him gently. "We have to see what happens next. Señora Lagrima is dead. That changes everything."

Alejandro pulled away. "She's not dead, she just left her body because it couldn't work anymore. Anyway, she wants us to stay in our cottage, she said so."

"Alejandro, I told you the cottage is not ours. It belongs to whoever inherits Señora Lagrima's hacienda, and I doubt they will care much about the daughter and grandson of the Señora's old manager."

"But Señora Lagrima told me if I lived to be eleven, I could have it!"

"If?" A burst of brittle laughter escaped Tia Lucia's lips. "Well then, on your eleventh birthday, perhaps we should return to claim it," she joked, blinking away a sudden flood of tears.

"That's in two months," said Alejandro gleefully. "Promise me!"

"Two and a half months, and I promise that whatever you wish from the bottom of your heart, you'll get. Now will you do as you're told? I have a feeling the troublemakers may come snooping around at the funeral day after tomorrow."

"They're coming today," Alejandro announced, and promptly turned and trotted off to the bathroom.

It usually took him a long time to bathe because he loved water so much, he would find reasons to stay until his fingers wrinkled up. He placed breadcrumbs on the windowsill for the ants, and while he waited for every morsel to be toted away, he washed his pyjamas, wrestling and bashing and stomping them clean. By the time he finally tiptoed out, dripping water all over the floor, his mother was inside fumbling around in his dresser. His backpack was on his bed already half-packed, and her own was on the floor, bulging with food, little cotton sacks of medicinal leaves, and clothing.

"Where's my whale and dolphin T-shirt?"

"It's packed. Dark colours are better for the trip," she murmured. "You saw them, didn't you?" she added, not looking up.

"Uh-huh." Alejandro pulled on the grey-brown T-shirt she laid out for him. "Last night my spirit visited the time to come and I saw two people with mean eyes and Agouti tattoos on their arms searching for us."

More and more often now, Alejandro's dreams were coming true.

"Then we must leave now."

"Cook and the others will worry if we just disappear," Alex reminded her.

Cook and two senior ranch hands had gone to buy new clothes for Señora Lagrima's funeral.

"Right." Tia Lucia strode purposefully into the kitchen. Alejandro hastily donned the matching track pants and followed. He watched as she scribbled in large letters: *'AWAY ON URGENT FAMILY BUSINESS – WILL RETURN AS SOON AS POSSIBLE',* and stuck the note on the fridge. "I have also left some of my special herbal remedies for them on the kitchen table," she added, "so perhaps they'll forgive us for leaving like this."

She went to the living room and lovingly removed the silver panman from its pedestal. It was the only memento Alejandro had of a father who was, according to the townsfolk, the best silversmith in all of South America.

Although the town was small, the people of Alma had a sense of great importance. Their town was on the border between Spanish and English South America, and many people met there to trade. Hordes of tourists came as well to watch the turtles nest. That was how the news spread about the little gift shop which belonged to Alejandro's father, Manuel Van Sertima. People who bought his silverwork swore there was magic in them. Visitors especially loved the silver panman, which he kept on display. Yet no one could persuade him to part with it, or even to craft another.

"Tell me again how Papi came to make the silver panman," Alejandro begged.

Tia Lucia blew gently on the figurine, and for a moment it seemed to come to life. *Plonk, plonk, plink, plonk*, played the panman. Her face relaxed into a tender smile.

"When Papi was a little boy, he went to visit the big city with Grandpapi. Being a stray like you, he decided

9

to go off exploring, while Grandpapi was taking care of business. As he was passing a grand building with arches and stone pillars, the sweetest sound of music caught his ears. Itching with curiosity, Papi followed the sound up the broad stairs, but before he could pry open the heavy door, an attendant stopped him. 'It's the mayor's annual Angels of Charity luncheon,' she told Papi. 'No one is allowed in without a ticket.'

"Well," Tia Lucia continued, "you can imagine Papi's disappointment. Angels had come down to earth to play, and the attendant wouldn't even let him have a peep. Sitting on a bench outside, he noticed the music was having a magical effect on passers-by. The anger of two lovers melted into smiles. An old man, bent over with worries, straightened and began to chip and sway in time to the beat. Papi wished he had the power to make people happy like that. Life in Alma was hard at the time," Tia Lucia explained. "Anyway, Papi lay down and closed his eyes. As his mind drifted, the music seemed to draw closer … and closer … and closer … until suddenly it was upon him, and then it stopped.

"Startled, Papi sat up. There, before him, stood an hombre with a fluffy salt and pepper beard. Hanging from his neck was a shiny spider pan, just like this one." Tia Lucia tapped the silver figurine. "Papi said the hombre's eyes twinkled and when he spoke, his chocolate brown face shone with mirth. 'I came,' he said, 'because you wished for it … and because I hadn't the heart to let you go on thinking panmen were angels."

Tia Lucia chuckled. "It was the first time Papi ever heard steel band music from the island across the gulf. The hombre explained how pans are made, how they sink them into a bowl shape and put in the notes. Papi listened attentively and then picked up a clump of mud and fashioned a pan out of it. The hombre was impressed. 'Manuel,' he said, 'you're very good with your hands.' Instantly, Papi shook his head. 'Everyone says I'm clumsy,' he said. 'Well,' said the hombre, 'the next time someone says that, you tell them Hamma said you'll make magic one day,' and with a wave, he was gone.

"At first, not many people took Papi's story seriously because, as it turned out, the maestro they call Hamma left Mother Earth the year before Papi met him. But when Papi crafted this exquisite silver figurine at age twelve, people began to believe. Papi always said the silver panman had a special purpose. He didn't know what until ..." Tia Lucia hesitated. "... until the end. He barely whispered, *'I know now! Let— panman—guide—'*, before he drew his final breath. You were just three, so you wouldn't remember."

"What did he mean?"

Tia Lucia shrugged. She handed the panman to Alejandro. "Place it among your clothes in the backpack. Make sure you—" She froze at the faint clanging of the front gate bell.

"They're here," said Alejandro. "We'll have to hide."

"No. We'll walk out of here under their noses."

"How?" Alejandro looked out. There were many trees in the courtyard but no undergrowth, just bare rust-coloured soil. "We can't get to the front gate without being seen."

"There are many ways to disappear," said Tia Lucia, with a determined glint in her eye. "We may wear European clothing and have African and European blood in our veins, but we are still Waspachus of the Cougar Clan, descendants of the Invisible People." The front gate bell jangled again. "Come."

She led Alejandro back to the bedroom, and as she watched him carefully tuck the panman between his clothes and secure the snaps on his backpack, she continued to speak quietly.

"We must be as stealthy as cougars, as still as rocks, and as swift as eagles. By the time the *bandidos* come around the great house to the back, we must be hidden among the trees, got that?"

Alejandro nodded.

"Are you sure? You must never look in their direction. Listen with your inner being. You will sense their movement when you become one with your surroundings."

"Right."

Tia Lucia smiled at his absolute confidence. "Okay. Tie your shoes to the strap of your backpack, and let's go. Once we're away from here, we'll use only our clan names, Alex Springfeather and Moon Woman. Another thing: let no one know of your powers unless you trust them completely."

Backpacks on, they slipped out the front door. Alejandro was about to bolt for the first line of trees, when he heard his mother murmur, "Walk swiftly and breathe lightly. Our noise must be no louder than the sound of the wind through the trees."

Going ahead of her, he cut through the garden and made a beeline for the trees furthest away from the path. They barely made it before two people, a man and a woman, came into view and stopped momentarily to look around. Dark glasses hid their eyes, but on their upper arms Alex could see clearly the Agouti tattoos. They were the people in his dream.

Standing very still, each beside a tree, Alejandro and Tia Lucia waited. All thoughts vanished from Alejandro's mind the moment he stopped looking, and listened. His breathing slowed. The sleeve of his shirt stirred in the wind as gently as a leaf on a branch. Suddenly he was no different from the tree, or the ant scurrying across his instep. He felt a faint tremor in the earth and stepped forward, sensing correctly the moment the Agouti people started along the path. Unnoticed, he and his mother slipped like shadows from tree to tree, drawing steadily closer to the great house.

Out of the blue, there was a sharp *SNAP!* Alejandro glanced in the direction of the sound and froze. It was Sasa, Cook's mischievous monkey. Trapped between trees, he watched in fascination as she raced along the ground straight for him. Time seemed to slow. The man and the woman peered suspiciously into the grove.

Draw in your energy now! a voice inside him whispered. He shifted his eyes away from the monkey immediately. "Energy, become small!" he commanded silently. Suddenly, the animal skidded to a halt, spun around once in confusion, then turned and scampered off in the opposite direction.

"Look at that!" the woman cried. "A baby monkey!"

"That's not a baby, that's a sakiwinki, and watch out, they like to bite," said the man sourly, and walked on. The woman followed hastily.

Alejandro breathed a tiny sigh of relief. Moving swiftly and noiselessly, he and Tia Lucia continued. Before long, they were at the front of the great brick house and through the gate.

Parked beside the driveway was the Agouti people's very snazzy blue SUV, and right across the road were the estate's cocoa and coconut fields. Beyond them was the fastest means of getting into town – the river. Señora Lagrima owned two canoes and a large speedboat. Alejandro would have loved to ride in the speedboat, but when they got down to the river, it was gone. Cook and the others had taken it. Quickly, they launched the larger of the two canoes and clambered in.

Alejandro had travelled in canoes since he was a baby, and paddled on his own since he was four. He and his mother made a good team. In no time at all, the fields were behind them. Paddling steadily, they entered the swamp. Two river dolphins wanted to race. As Alejandro and Tia Lucia swiftly rounded a bend, a frantic flapping of red feathers sounded an alarm. GWEE! GWEE! A flock of scarlet ibis rose into the air like a fiery cloud, parting just in time to let the canoe pass. Alejandro glanced back. The birds were already circling back to return to their feeding ground. This was the part of the river he loved best. The mangrove trees, with their roots above-ground, were like multi-legged giants guarding the forest. An otter interrupted his roll in the mud to whistle hello.

Alejandro waved back.

"Let's rest," he said breathlessly, laying his paddle down.

"Okay."

Tia Lucia had been eyeing him strangely since they started down the river, and now she blurted out, "How did you do that? How did you disappear completely in the grove?"

Alex grinned wickedly. "I'm a descendant of the Invisible People."

"Yes, but we become invisible by creating an illusion, Alex Springfeather."

"My wisdom voice told me to make my energy small, so I did it."

Tia Lucia was speechless for a moment. "Who is this soul sent to me by the Great Spirit?" she finally whispered.

"Ah, Mami, don't look so dopey. It was nothing."

"Nothing?" His mother giggled involuntarily. "You think other people can do that?"

Alex nodded confidently. "Señora Lagrima told me there are others like me. One day I'll find them."

A shadow crossed Tia Lucia's face. "I hope so," she muttered.

The sombreness which descended on her did not lift until they docked at Plaza de Coral. On the shore, beneath a string of fluttering yellow flags, a man with a cuatro and a woman with maracas were entertaining onlookers.

"Life is good, why worry?" said Tia Lucia, chipping to the calypso beat. She tripped on the uneven pier, and that put an end to that. Laughing, they headed for the town square.

"Where are we going now?" asked Alex eagerly.

"To visit a friend who lives along the coast."

Walking briskly past the shops filled with wickerwork, painted gourds and hammocks, they crossed the square and entered a side street where several colourful buses were parked. Despite the long queue, they managed to get seats together. The driver waited until all the passengers were in, and then hopped off the bus for a smoke. It was sweltering inside.

Alex leaned through the window, *"¡Frio-frio!"* The shave-ice man started towards him. A glint of silvery blue caught his eye. Instantly he ducked. A blue SUV cruised by and disappeared around the next corner.

"Is it them?" asked Tia Lucia anxiously. "Did they see us?"

Alex shrugged. He kept a wary eye out until the bus lumbered onto the coastal road, and then excitement took over. There was so much to see: seagulls squabbling over food, fried fish vendors hustling for customers, screaming boys and girls racing the blue-brown waves to shore … He hung out the rattling window until his eyes streamed. All too soon, the journey came to an end.

"Watch your step," the bus driver warned, as they hopped off the stairs onto a beach beside a sign that said, Villa del Corazon.

"Well, our grand adventure begins," said Tia Lucia gaily.

"I was thinking the same thing too," said Alex happily.

As the bus pulled off, their faces fell. The strand was grungy. Groups of rowdy tourists lolled around on rickety beach chairs drinking and gambling. Across the road, beyond the steady stream of traffic, a hotel proclaimed itself to be the Corazon Ritz. The sign was propped up against a peeling wall near its dingy entrance.

Alex screwed up his face disappointedly. "I don't like this town."

"When one door closes, another is sure to open, but the oddest adventures often lie in between," said Tia Lucia with a chuckle. "So let us see what's in store for us." Shielding her eyes from the midday sun, she looked up the dusty road. Her gaze settled on a fried chicken shop. "Ah, there's Freda's. My friend is about twenty minutes walk from there. Want some *pollo frito* first?"

"Uh-huh. I'm hungry."

Half way to Freda's Fried Chicken, Tia Lucia suddenly stopped. "Wait here. I want to buy something."

Across the road was a quirky gadget shop, sandwiched between a dreary tailor shop and a dinky little restaurant. *WIDGETS OF THE WORLD*, a cracked sign said.

"Why can't I come? We have to cross the road anyway."

"I'm going to get your birthday present."

In the window of the shop, there were things whizzing around and hopping up and down and bobbing left and right. Alex's eyes gleamed. "Okay."

Tia Lucia dashed across the road, turned and waved, grinning mischievously. A truck roared sluggishly by, blowing sand in Alex's face. By the time the air cleared, his mother was gone. Alex found a flat rock on the beach. The moment he sat down, he caught a glimpse of a tall man eyeing him from behind a makeshift fish stall. A straw hat partially hid his features. Something about him made Alex uneasy. Nearby, some fishermen were mending their nets. He decided to while away the time with them. They regaled him with stories of red snappers gigantic enough to capsize a boat, and four-eyed fish that warned of storms. Their yarns were interlaced with raucous laughter and back slapping, as each tried to outdo the other.

Out of the blue, a terrible feeling gripped Alex. With a quick goodbye, he raced across the road, dodging between the cars and trucks. There were many interesting things on tables and shelves and hanging on the walls of the gadget shop, but Alex could think only of searching behind and under the mountainous jumble for his mother.

"The lady in the brownish dress, with the long plaits, and the backpack," he gestured frantically to the shop attendant, "did you see where she went?"

The man shrugged disinterestedly.

A fat bespectacled woman fiddling with a springy thingamabob overheard. She turned and said kindly, "I saw her go into the restaurant next door. Such a nice lady. She held the door for me, but the man she was with …" She snorted and turned away.

A now frantic Alex shot out of the shop, almost overturning a stand crawling with metal ants. The adjoining restaurant had no name, no customers, and after rapping several times on the soiled counter, Alex concluded that there was no waitress or cook either. He checked every shop on the strip. He stopped and asked people along the way. No one could remember seeing his mother.

He returned to the rock and sat down. Covering his eyes lightly with his fingers, he tried to imagine where she could be. It was a game they had started playing recently, and he always won. For all his efforts, though, all he could see was a vision of her vanishing in a cloud of dust. Suddenly, he felt a presence. Dropping his hands, he opened his eyes to find a grimfaced policewoman glaring down at him.

"You waiting for someone?" she barked in a gravelly voice.

Alex eyed her warily. "Yes, my mother. She went to the store."

"A young beggar tried to steal from one of the shops over there." She leaned over him menacingly. "He matches your description. Was it you? And don't try to lie because I can see it in your face."

Alex slid off the rock away from her. "I'm not a beggar. I came with my mother to Corazon to visit a friend."

"Who? Give me a name."

He shrugged.

"You beggars are all liars and thieves," the policewoman sneered. "That's why we don't want you here."

"I told you I'm not a beggar," said Alex, stamping his foot angrily. "Look! There are some beggars over there." He pointed towards a man and a young boy by the water's edge pressing a scraggy looking foreigner for money. "Why don't you ask them?"

The policewoman scowled. "You want to tell me how to do my job? Alright, come with me."

For the first time in his life, Alex's confidence deserted him. Desperate, he made a dash for the road. A man in plainclothes jumped out of a police car and intercepted him, grabbing him by the arm. Alex struggled to get away. A crowd began to gather as the police forced Alex towards the car.

"WAIT!" Alex yelled. "YOU DON'T UNDERSTAND! I'M NOT A THIEF! MY MO—" The man clapped a hand over his mouth, shoved him in the back seat and sat down heavily beside him. "HELP!" Alex cried out hopelessly, as a crowd of sympathetic faces surrounded the vehicle.

The policewoman slid behind the wheel, turned the siren on and the crowd scattered. Speeding off, she turned the corner after Freda's Fried Chicken and headed inland. Wild-eyed, Alex tried to memorize street signs, but the man kept yanking him away from the window. The car turned left, then right, then left again. Eventually, it pulled up before a tall wooden building painted a sickly yellow. CORAZON BOYS' HOME, a sign said. It was surrounded by a high corrugated zinc fence and had a strong iron gate with a huge padlock. The gate was ajar.

Quickly the man got out, dragging Alex with him.

"Where are you taking me?" Alex croaked, hoarse from yelling.

"You'll stay here until we find your mother. If you try to resist, we'll throw you in jail instead. Here you are, matron, all yours," he called out to a massive woman approaching. Her arms were as big as a stevedore's and her beady eyes were as cold as ice. Shoving Alex through the gate and tossing his backpack after him, the man pulled it shut and secured it with the padlock.

The matron grabbed Alex by the collar and hauled him and his backpack towards the stairs of the boys' home. He could hear the police laughing as the car pulled away.

"When my mother finds out about this, all of you are going to be in big trouble!" Alex threatened.

"Oh shut up about your mother," said the matron callously. "It's obvious she doesn't want you anymore. That's why you're here. It happens all the time."

"THAT'S NOT TRUE!" Alex roared. "SHE WENT TO GET MY BIRTHDAY PRESENT. LET ME GO!"

Twisting and tugging, he slipped out of his shirt and out of the matron's clutches. Just as he turned to run, a wave of water knocked him to his knees.

"That ought to cool him down," said a mean voice.

Coughing and spluttering, Alex looked up. A woman in an apron was standing at the head of the short flight of stairs with an empty bucket in her hands. She bore a striking resemblance to the matron in size and shape.

"Well done, cook," said the matron approvingly.

Bedraggled, Alex allowed himself to be led inside. They marched him through an enormous room with three long tables and chairs, and down a corridor to the kitchen. The cook left them at this point. The matron led him outside to a long shed behind the building. She flung the doors open. Alex gasped. There were sewing machines everywhere, and behind them were children stitching away furiously. It was stuffy inside. A boy of no more than six jumped up. Quickly, he covered his machine with a box and placed a plant on top.

The matron was beside him in a flash. "Does he look like an inspector to you?" she growled, slapping him upside his head. "Get back to work!" Turning to Alex, she said, "This is where you'll earn your keep."

She closed the doors and marched him back into the main building. Down the corridor they went to a flight of worn wooden stairs.

"Up, up," she growled.

Alex climbed the stairs to a second level, with the matron at his heels. She shoved him into a dormitory with rows and rows of empty beds, and kept poking him with a finger in the back until they came to the middle of the room.

"Here is your bed and your side table. Your cake of soap has to last two months, and your towel and toothbrush, a year, so don't lose them. I will give you today off, since this is your first day," the matron continued, "but from tomorrow, you'll have to pull your weight like everyone else." Alex barely heard the list of rules she rattled off. "Now get out of those wet clothes and take a shower at the end of the corridor," she ordered and trod heavily away.

Alex dropped his backpack on the floor. His bed was close to one of the windows facing the road. In the empty lot opposite, fields of tall grass blew freely in the wind. He stared longingly past the bars. "I'll get out. I know I will," he muttered, glaring down at the padlocked gate.

Throwing himself on the bed in the same wet clothes, he imagined himself walking out the gate. Over and over, he played the scene in his mind, like a movie, until his eyelids began to droop. He fought to stay awake but eventually lost the battle.

A raucous argument woke him. He jumped up and looked around in dismay. It was not a nightmare. The orphanage, the lumpy bed, were real. Alex gazed out. The sun was dipping below the trees. He must have slept for hours. The place was eerily quiet except for the screeching coming from below. There was no sign of the other children yet. His eyes fell on the gate, and for a moment he dared not breathe. It was still shut, but someone had left the padlock undone!

With not a moment to waste, he took off his runners, tied them to his backpack, shrugged it on and quickly headed for the stairs. At the bottom, he peered around the banister down the corridor. The matron and the cook were in the kitchen abusing a man. He looked like a handyman. Freedom was just a few feet away, but Alex was beginning to have second thoughts. If he failed, he knew he could expect no mercy from either woman.

Walk swiftly, breathe lightly, he heard his mother murmur.

Remembering, Alex drew himself up. Courage took the place of fear. He slipped across the corridor into the big hall and headed silently for the front door. Opening it and closing it gently behind him, Alex rushed to the gate, removed the heavy padlock and stepped out. When he replaced the padlock, he snapped it shut.

He ran and ran and did not stop until he was well away. He retraced his steps from memory. All the way, he imagined seeing his mother on the beach. By early evening, he was back near the area where he was captured.

Night was kinder to Corazon. Campfires dotted the strand, creating a mysterious aura. The drunken singing and laughter, and clinking beer bottles were a reminder of where he was. A man kicked a young beggar in his stomach and his friends roared with laughter. Alex scuttled away. He walked up and down the beach, checking the shadows, calling for his mother softly, even though he knew the moment he arrived that she was not there. A loneliness and desolation overcame him. He sat down on the grubby sand and stared blindly out to sea.

"There you are!" a voice behind him said jovially, making him jump.

Alex glanced back. A dark-complexioned youth of about fifteen or sixteen was standing a few feet away. He sported a bandana tied rakishly over his unkempt curly hair, a tattoo of a snake on his left arm and an earring in one ear. With his turned up pants and green-striped muscle shirt, Alex thought he was a pirate.

"Are you talking to me?"

"Course, who else?"

Alex stiffened. "What do you want?"

"An angel sent me to watch over you." The youth grinned disarmingly. "I am Rico Marquez, who are you?" Alex hesitated. "You don't have to worry," Rico added, "you're safe with me."

Alex decided to trust him, even though he looked dodgy. "My name is Alex Springfeather."

"That's right, I remember now," said Rico, throwing himself on the sand beside him. "That's what the angel said. Go to the filthiest beach in Corazon, and you will find a drooping feather without a spring in it."

Alex broke into laughter. "Are you from Corazon?"

"Not me." As he spoke, Rico observed a group of drunken men and women making signs to a bewildered fisherman. *"Kan ik helpen?"* he called out. One of the men staggered towards him. *"Het zal u kosten,"* Rico added quickly. The man nodded.

Rico whipped out a pad from a knee pocket and wrote as the man spoke. He handed the note to the man. In return, the man gave him money.

"You know those people?" asked Alex curiously.

"No. Don't have to. People tell me what they want, I translate. It's a good way to make a quick buck. I can do that in five languages," Rico boasted.

A couple came up to him and murmured something.

Rico frowned. *"Comment cela?"*

Without thinking, Alex explained what they meant.

Rico shot him a startled glance. "Oh." He turned back to the couple with a forced cocky grin. *"Alors, mes amis, je suis votre homme – pour des dollars."*

The couple paid for the translation and departed.

Rico eyed Alex, slightly put out. "You didn't tell me you could speak French."

"French?" Alex gaped. "I— I guess I forgot that I knew it." He lowered his eyes guiltily. Instinctively he knew this was not the time or the place to talk about his growing powers.

"Hmm. So what's a smart *niño* like you doing on this crazy beach alone?"

By the end of Alex's tale, Rico's irritation vanished completely.

"Whew! What rotten luck!" he said. "Good thing the handyman left the gate open. Your mother must be around somewhere. Tomorrow, I'll help you find her, and if those mangy goats from the orphanage try to capture you again, they'll have to deal with me!"

"Thanks, Rico," said Alex, brightening up. "I'll give you money for your help."

Rico looked stunned. "I am doing this out of kindness, and you think I am doing it *por dineros*?" he gasped. "I demand an apology!"

"I'm sorry!" said Alex, shaken.

Rico inclined his head graciously. "Apology accepted. If, of course, your *mother* wants to offer money," he added, "I'll not be so rude as to refuse."

His eyes were twinkling, and Alex realized that Rico was not to be taken seriously. The makeshift fish stall on the beach was still open. Rico treated Alex to a meal, and Alex treated him to drinks from his pocket money. While they ate, Rico talked about the boat he would buy when he got rich, and Alex talked about the cottage that would be his on his eleventh birthday.

When at length Alex asked Rico what time he had to go home, Rico guffawed. "I *am* home. You're sitting in my living room!"

Alex sniggered. "You don't live on the beach."

"Why not? I like to be as free as a bird." A sly look appeared on Rico's face. "If you want, you can stay and work with me until your mother shows up. You'll need money for food."

"Okay," Alex agreed readily, not knowing what he was getting himself into.

The next day and the next, they combed Corazon looking for Tia Lucia, while Rico taught Alex the art of hustling. Corazon, like Alma, was not a very big town, yet Tia Lucia seemed to have vanished into thin air.

On the third day of their search, after a spot of trouble with the law over a watch, which a tourist claimed had been stolen, but which Rico insisted had been payment for a job, Rico decided to pull up stakes.

"You know what?" he said to Alex, "I'll tell you what happened: while you were at the orphanage, your mother came back. She knew you didn't know the way to her friend, so where would you go without her? Back to Alma. I bet she's there in that nice cottage you told me about!"

Alex's eyes lit up. "Of course, that's what happened!"

That day, they took a bus to Plaza de Coral and then another to Señora Lagrima's hacienda. The bus deposited them at the head of the lane and Alex, impatient to get there, ran all the way up. When he arrived, he found the gate chained and padlocked. Never in his life had he seen a lock on the gate. Puzzled, he shook the bell.

"Hoy! What have we here?" said Rico, coming up and shaking the chain.

Alex shook the bell again, but no one came. It was strangely quiet inside. No clucking chickens, no chattering monkey, no lilting songs from cook as she washed the dishes.

"We have to climb over the gate," said Alex determinedly.

"Why waste time? Tia Lucia cannot be here," Rico reasoned.

"But what if she left a note for me in our cottage?" Alex's voice rose in desperation.

"Okay, okay."

Together they climbed over the six foot iron gate easily and made their way to the cottage. It was securely locked as well. Alex peered through a window. Everything was gone. His home had been stripped bare.

On their way back to town, Alex spoke little. Rico stayed quiet too out of sympathy. But when they stepped off the bus near Plaza de Coral, he decided enough was enough.

"My mother ran away too," he declared, "and here I am, doing very well. So forget about it, and let's have some fun."

Alex rounded on him. "MY MOTHER DID NOT RUN AWAY!" he yelled in Rico's face.

Rico ducked away in surprise. "Okay, Okay. Don't get frisky, *niño*, my mother didn't either. I just said that to cheer you up."

Sulking, Alex walked away. Rico trailed behind. The sun had set, the shops were closed and street lights were on.

In the centre of the town square, Alex stopped abruptly. "Mother Hen!" he shouted, his face radiant with excitement. "I forgot about Mother Hen!"

Rico arched an eyebrow in surprise. "You forgot about a chicken? Is it a pet, or can we eat it?"

"Don't be silly, Mother Hen is Maria! She's my mother's friend and she works at night in the bakery across the street *there*." Alex was positively hopping up and down as he pointed to a little shop with cakes in the window. "She'll know where Mami is!"

"Then let's go find her. I hope she's young and sexy," Rico added, rolling his eyes and shaking his hips comically, but Alex was already halfway across the street.

As soon as they rapped on the backdoor of the bakery, it opened and a kindly face peered out.

"Alex, my little chick, how nice to see you!" Maria flung the door open and wrapped him in her ample arms. She was dressed in white as usual, from her turban to her shoes, and her ebony cheeks were smudged with flour. "Where is Tia Lucia, and who is this nice young man?"

Alex looked into her smoky-grey eyes. "Didn't my mother come to see you?" His eyes begged her to say yes.

"Good heavens, no! I haven't seen her since the day of old Señora Lagrima's death!"

Alex fought back the tears, but they flooded his eyes anyway. The expression on Maria's face changed from puzzlement to concern.

"Come, come, child." She hustled them into the back of the bakery where the bags of flour were stored and sat Alex down on the only chair. "Tell me what happened," she demanded, perching on a nearby flour bag.

Alex poured out his story and she tut-tutted all through, tears filling her eyes as well.

"You think the Agouti people took your mother, no?" she asked finally.

Alex nodded.

"Well, I don't. Tia Lucia is too clever by half. There must be a simple explanation. Give me a week and I'll find her." She rose. "Now, let's find you somewhere to stay. I wish I could take you in, but my landlord is mean."

"He can stay with me," Rico offered, stepping forward. He had been wandering around behind the bags of flour. "I'll take care of him like a brother."

"Oh!" Maria had forgotten he was there. "And who might you be?"

"This is Rico Marquez. He speaks five languages and makes money translating for people," said Alex with a touch of pride. "He's helping me find Mami."

Maria looked him up and down. "You don't have a penny, do you?" she said shrewdly. Rico shook his head. "Perhaps I can get you a job delivering for the bakery, but until then, try the old beach cabanas out by the dump. You're sure to find something there. Make sure you get one with a good roof."

As the two stepped out the backdoor, Maria grabbed some empty flour bags and stuffed them in Alex's arms. "For bedding. Does he know about your powers?" she whispered, gesturing at Rico's disappearing back.

Alex shook his head.

"Good. The panman, *you* have it, I trust?"

Alex jabbed his backpack.

"Clever girl, Lucia," Maria breathed. "Guard it with your life."

RAINBOWS AND OTHER
STRANGE SIGNS

ON THEIR FIRST DAY AWAY FROM THEIR NEW BEACH HOME, someone stole their belongings. That same evening, seeing a flickering light a stone's throw away, Alex and Rico went and knocked on the door of a cabana with shrubs growing on its roof.

"There are only six of us here, including you," said their neighbour Carpo The Butcher, whose name had nothing to do with meat, and everything to do with the way he butchered people's gardens. Carpo, who weeded for a living, was a big, kindly man, but his eyes were crossed and he was no good at handling delicate things like flowers. Carpo hung his lantern on the doorjamb. "It was not me, or Café or Flor," he pointed over his shoulder to a skinny couple sitting in the shadows.

"We saw Rojo The Rake Thief sniffing around here," said the woman named Flor.

Café shook his head in agreement. "I bet he did it."

"We'll help you get them back," said Carpo.

Outside the door of Rojo's cabana, Flor began to have second thoughts. "What if he—"

A floorboard creaked. The front door began to rattle and heave, and the whole structure shuddered. Strong winds had twisted the cabana into a zigzag.

Everyone stepped back in case it collapsed, but Rojo finally got the door open. He was tall, with a stoop. His sunken eyes were filled with loathing. Alex shuddered.

"WHAT?"

Carpo did not beat about the bush. "We've come for the stuff you stole from these boys' cabana."

"Well, you came to the wrong place." Rojo looked down his nose at Alex and Rico. "Why would I steal from a pair of monkeys like them? Do I look like a person who likes peanuts?"

Actually in his moth-eaten black suit, he looked like somebody had just died, and smelled as if that person was him.

"You should stick to stealing people's rakes and selling them back to them," said Flor sternly, wiggling a pale finger at him. "Life is hard enough without us stealing from each other."

"Let's search the zigzag," Café urged, edging forward with the upheld lantern.

Rojo's face turned purple. "If anyone dares to enter my home, I'll whack them with this!" he growled, brandishing a rake he was hiding behind his back.

Taken by surprise, they tumbled over each other to get out of his way. Encouraged, Rojo charged at them, swinging the rake wildly, and everyone turned and ran, with Flor leading the way and Rico bringing up the rear. Halfway to the water's edge, Rico suddenly stopped and turned. The startled Rojo almost barrelled into him. Rico nimbly stepped aside, snatched the rake from him with ease and tossed it to the ground.

"If you ever threaten me or my brother again, I'll whack you with *this*," he said, shoving his fist menacingly in Rojo's face. Rojo took one look at Rico's rippling muscles, spied the mad glint in his eye and turned to flee. He stepped on the rake. The handle flew up and smacked him right on the nose. Roaring with pain, he grabbed the rake and bolted back to his hut. Everyone collapsed with laughter.

"He's guilty alright," Café gasped. "See the way his bushy brows quivered at the thought of a search? Let's go back. Who knows how long he'll be in the zigzag this time. He disappears for weeks, sometimes months. No one knows where he goes."

"Forget it," said Alex, sobering up. "We have what we need." He patted his backpack gratefully. The silver panman was still there, wrapped in his favourite whale and dolphin T-shirt.

"That stinky suit he wears every day." Flor wrinkled her nose. "It's all his greedy brother left behind when he ran off with the family inheritance years ago. Poor Rojo."

"Poor nothing. He has a mean streak," Carpo warned. "You boys, watch out for him."

They did, but their paths rarely crossed his. While Rojo seemed to prefer to keep out of sight, Alex and Rico got about.

"Today will be a good day, I predict," Rico declared every morning on their way to town. And it would always turn out to be. They ran errands for sunbathers, they helped tag turtles, and every now and then, Rico would make some extra money translating for traders. When the blazing midday sun chased the tourists and wildlife conservationists indoors, Rico and Alex would head for Punto del Cielo. This was a rough neighbourhood on the other side of town, where the loggers and miners hung out. There they would listen to dramatic tales of life deep in the jungle, and do odd jobs for them.

At the end of the week, on Saturday evening, Maria came to visit. Alex was playing cards by moonlight with Rico and Carpo, and bopping to music. The moment he saw her face, however, he froze.

"Something very strange is going on, my little chick," Maria murmured, accepting the rickety stool Carpo vacated. "I can find no trace of Tia Lucia. Nothing."

"Did you talk to the chief?" asked Carpo, eager to help. "They say he has high contacts in low places."

Maria frowned uneasily. "Yes I did speak to the police chief. A slacker if ever I saw one. 'Why should I bother myself?' he said. 'The witness at the gadget store as good as said that she ran off with a m—'" Maria clapped a hand to her mouth and shot a glance at Alex, who was hanging on her every word.

"But she didn't run away," he said tightly.

Maria put her arms around him and gave him a squeeze. She smelled of vanilla. "I know. He was being mean – asking questions about you all the time instead of getting out there and searching for Tia Lucia. 'Does the boy seem normal?' he kept asking like a stuck record."

Rico burst into laughter. "You can tell him that the boy squiggles strange signs in the sand in his sleep. That's *definitely* not normal."

"No I don't."

"Yes, you do, *niño*."

"What kind of signs?" asked Carpo curiously.

And Rico squiggled something with his toe.

"What is it?" Carpo squinted. "A two-headed boa that just swallowed a donkey?"

Alex gazed at it. "It's the sign we saw on the ground beside Señora Lagrima's cane! The one everybody says is the mark of her killer!" he exclaimed in amazement. "What does it mean, Mother Hen?"

"I don't know," said Maria, in wonderment. "Your mother would know such things."

"She would? But she never said anything to me or to cook, or to anybody."

"Nor would I if I thought something strange was afoot. Can you *see* her?" she asked softly, suddenly changing tack.

A looked passed between them. Alex knew immediately what she meant. He shook his head. "I can't. I don't know why."

"Hmmm." Maria pursed her lips. "In that case, I think we must move fast. The police chief was very interested in your whereabouts. Too interested, considering that he did not intend to help."

Rico turned the music down. "Mother Hen, please tell me you did not give him my name," he pleaded.

Maria's eyes narrowed. "That is a very fancy music box you have there," she said coolly, eying it. "Did you turn down the delivery job at the bakery to steal, Rico?"

"We don't steal," said Alex proudly, "we make a lot of money running errands."

"Not that much," said Maria tartly.

"Just tell me, did you call my name?" asked Rico in an agitated voice. "Did you say where we live?"

"No, I said the boy is staying with his grandparents, so you are safe."

"But I don't have grandparents," said Alex grinning.

"I know. I told them a lie." Maria sighed. "The sooner we find Tia Lucia, the better for my soul, and there is only one person left to turn to: Grandfather Talking Dove. No one sees him unless he wants them to, and no one knows exactly where he is, but perhaps he might come out of hiding for you. We must think of a way to get a message to him."

"Are you out of your mind?" croaked Carpo. "You want to send our young friend to a certain death?"

Alex looked from one to the other in confusion. "Who is Grandfather Talking Dove?"

"A powerful medicine man who lives in Cree Kee Forest," whispered Carpo, his voice trembling with terror. "No one is allowed to destroy that forest – it is a reserve, so he can hide there in peace and wait for poor souls to stumble upon his lair. Then with his eyes, he brings death upon them. But before that, he plucks a poisonous feather from his headdress and tortures them."

"Old men's tales!" said Maria, scowling at Carpo, "Pay no attention, my little chick."

"Jaime The Tailor's son turned green and died three days after seeing the medicine man," said Carpo defensively.

"Yes, but—"

"And old man Juan wrinkled up like a prune and died one day after seeing him."

"But that had nothing to do with—"

A most unusual sound from Alex stopped Maria. She stared at him in consternation. The blood had drained from his face. "What's the matter?"

"Someone will try to kill me. I'm sure of it now. I don't know if it will be the Agouti people or the medicine man in Cree Kee Forest. All I know is Señora Lagrima is dead, maybe Mami is dead, and I'm next."

"Don't ever say that again!" said Maria sternly. "Your mother is *not* dead, and no one is going to kill you, least of all Grandfather Talking Dove. He may be peculiar, but he's not a bad man."

"The axe of death hangs over Alex's head and you want to hand him over to the woodsman," said Carpo accusingly.

"The medicine man can help," Maria insisted stubbornly. "He has the power to see what many others can't. Are you willing to try him, Alex?"

Alex screwed up his face and shook his head. "Not me."

Maria drew a ragged breath. "Then I don't know what else to suggest ..."

"I'll make as much money as I can," said Alex with renewed determination, "and then I'll search every town until I find her."

"Good, I'm game," said Rico, twitching eagerly.

"Alex, be patient, my little chick. Give me one more week. I will meditate and pray. Something is bound to come to me."

Soon thereafter, Maria left.

And then the rains came. Rivulets of water ran through the streets of Alma, the sea raged and the bullfrogs croaked non-stop in delight. The tourists were the first to leave, then the traders and finally the loggers and the miners, who preferred to wait out the rains in the big city. Only the wildlife conservationists remained.

Money was hard to come by. Some days all Alex and Rico had to eat was a small patty or cheese roll, and they had to beg to get them. Maria could not be found. Her modest home on the edge of town was locked up tightly. According to her supervisor at the bakery, she was "away".

Two torrential weeks passed. Their cabana roof did not leak, but the sunken floor, which was more sand than wood, felt damp all the time. Alex stormed down to the water's edge. "You have to stop!" he shouted at the rain. "You are ruining my life! How can I find my mother without money? I want her back! I want a nice home with food and chairs and a real bed! I don't want to live here anymore!"

The following day, the sun came out.

It was destined to be a strange day from start to finish. Rico predicted this the moment he looked up from his sandy bed and saw sunlight filtering through a tiny hole above his head.

"Oh no," he moaned, shaking Alex awake. "No money, no food, and now the roof has sprung a leak. No good will come of today, I can feel it."

"I had a strange dream," Alex murmured drowsily. "I'm running and running, and there's a fire."

"Well," said Rico dryly. "It figures. It wouldn't surprise me a bit if someone knocked at the door and said, 'You no longer have a town to go to. The sun came out, and not being used to it, Alma burned down.'"

THUMP! THUMP!

Startled, both Alex and Rico sat bolt upright and stared at the door.

THUMP! THUMP!

Carpo and Café and Flor usually tapped on the window. Who could it be?

Rico jumped up, pushed away the heavy crate which held the door shut and looked outside. He looked left, then right, then left again.

"It's the strangest thing," he said, leaving the door ajar and sitting down on the crate with a dazed expression. "There's a donkey outside with a rainbow painted on its forehead."

Alex sprang up to look. The donkey nibbled placidly at a cluster of wild flowers by the door. "That's not a rainbow. Can't have a rainbow without blue."

"And that's not all," Rico continued as if he hadn't heard Alex, "there's a rainbow above his head."

Cocking an eyebrow, Alex looked again. "The rainbow is out at sea, Rico. Rainbows always come out when sun follows rain. Did Carpo get a donkey? Is business picking up?"

"That donkey is a sign," said Rico, as if in a trance. "Perhaps we should not go out today."

Alex sniggered. "Chicken."

"CHICKEN!" Rico roared, coming alive. He sprang up. "WHO ARE YOU CALLING CHICKEN?"

Half an hour later, they were walking along the shoreline on their way to town. Around the halfway point, a huge wave suddenly came out of nowhere and dumped an enormous sea creature right across their path.

"¡Aiiii!" Alex shrieked, as the two startled friends scattered in different directions. "It almost got me! … What is it?"

It lay there motionless, like a large, colourful balloon with streamers attached.

"I don't know." Rico grabbed a stick and edged forward cautiously. He poked it. The colours pulsated like neon lights, but the creature did not stir.

"It looks like a monster jellyfish; is it a monster jellyfish?"

"Never seen a jellyfish like that!" Rico prodded again.

"Watch out, it's moving!" Alex dashed for safety.

Rico sprinted for higher ground just as another huge wave came crashing in and swept the creature back out. The two friends stood transfixed as it bobbed further and further out.

"Th-that was the third sign, *niño*! Th-three rainbows in a row!" Rico spluttered, barely able to contain himself.

"Phuh!" Alex dismissed Rico's pronouncement. "The monster jellyfish had even less colours than the donkey. In any case, Mami said strange things get tossed out of the sea when a big storm is coming."

"Take a look, *niño*. The sun is shining and the sky is clear. It's a sign."

As they neared the edge of town, they heard the distant meh-eh-eh-ing of goats tumbling through the tangle of roadside bushes. Maria's goats have started to stray, thought Alex sadly. They must be starving.

"Oooh, my little chick, thank God you're safe!" gushed a breathless voice from behind. *"Come quickly!"*

Alex turned. Maria emerged from the path through the bushes. "Mother Hen! You went away and didn't tell us," Alex scolded, before realizing that one of her hands was bandaged and there were bruises on her face. "What happened? Did you have an accident? Were you in hospital?"

Maria hauled him behind a sea grape tree. "I saw you coming and came to warn you. I cannot talk for long, it's not safe." Her voice rose to a feverish pitch. "I'm sorry, my little chick. I told them where you are! I had to, otherwise the kidnappers would have wrung my neck!"

"What's going on?" asked Rico, coming up. "What kidnappers?"

"Shhhh!" Maria grabbed his arm desperately. "You must leave Alma today! Promise me you won't let

42

anything happen to my little chick." Rico stared into her gaunt face, speechless. *"Promise me!"* she rasped, squeezing his arm tighter.

"OW! I promise."

Maria pressed an empanada into each of their hands and kissed them both. "God bless you and keep you safe."

Stunned, Alex watched her disappear up the path. "It's them, the Agouti people."

"Madre de ladrónes," whispered Rico, rubbing the arm she had gripped. "Poor Maria! What did you do to those people, *niño?"*

"Nothing." Alex swung in his direction, his expression wild. "I didn't do anything, Rico! It's all Señora Lagrima's fault for dying!"

"Perhaps they think you saw something."

"Well, I didn't. How are we going to leave? We have no bus fare."

A determined look came over Rico's face. "Just do as I say, and we'll be out of here before you can say 'baboon'!"

Rico marched Alex towards Alma's only three-star hotel, which stood across the road from its best beach. It was still quite early, around six forty-five in the morning, and at first the beach appeared deserted.

"Hoy!" Rico suddenly exclaimed, grabbing Alex by the arm. "That pretty lady in the bikini sitting in the shallows. She left her radio on her beach towel. It's small enough to fit under my shirt. You talk to her, and I'll do the rest. Remember, never give your real name to a mark."

"You're going to steal from her?" said Alex in dismay.

"*We're* going to steal from her," Rico corrected firmly.

Suddenly there was a sharp clap of thunder. Alex glanced back. Storm clouds were gathering, and the wind was picking up. "I think it's a bad idea. Let's just ask her for money."

"And if she says no, what then? Do you see anyone else around? Just go. Go, now, while she's busy!"

The woman sat with her back to them looking down at something. Rico stayed well back while Alex made his way over. Both his English and his Spanish were good. Senora Lagrima saw to that. "You are the bridge between the two lands, remember that," she used to say. But tourists were more easily charmed by pidgin English.

"Goo-day, Señora. 'Ow-a-you?" he started off haltingly.

The woman looked up. *"Buenos dias, amigo,"* she said, smiling sweetly.

Alex almost panicked. *"Habla usted español, Señora?"*

She shook her head ruefully, and her afro-puffs bobbed merrily around her ears. "Only a little. *Pocito.*"

He breathed a silent sigh of relief. A *Norteamenicana.* Latin American tourists were not easy to impress. "You look for *concha*?"

The woman frowned briefly. "You mean shells? Yes, I'm looking for shells." She eyed him quizzically. "You want to help me?"

"Oh yes, please."

Eagerly, Alex took off his sneakers and waded into the water. Out of the corner of his eye he could see Rico sidling towards them.

"Did you come for an early morning swim too?" asked the lady, dog-paddling in the air.

"No— ah— I sweem ago."

"You mean you've finished swimming."

"*Si si*, feeneesh sweem. Sorry, Engleesh no good."

Rico was just a few paces away now.

"It's much better than my Spanish, my dear. I'm very impressed." Her voice had gone all mushy. "Did your mo— *wooaaah*..."

A wind-whipped wave almost toppled them over. The woman threw her head back and giggled like a little girl. Alex could not take his eyes off her happy, sapodilla brown face. Her eyes sparkled like his mother's.

"You verrry booteeful, Señora," he said wistfully. "Just like mine mother."

"Wow, thanks!" The woman beamed. A couple of drops fell on her eyelids. "Rain!" she exclaimed, "I think you'd better run home now, or you'll get soaked."

With that she rolled onto her knees and turned, catching Rico in the act. "Hey, YOU!" she yelled, rising swiftly and sprinting towards him. She moved with long, graceful strides, like an athlete. From the direction of the hotel, a burly man in a brown suit also started running towards Rico. He had an umbrella in one hand and was holding the top of his head with the other.

45

Alex's stomach lurched. "Drop it, Rico, drop it!" he begged silently.

Rico looked from one to the other, backed away slowly, then dropped the radio and bolted.

Alex grabbed his sneakers and was by the lady's side in a flash. "I call *policia*, get bad hombre," he offered breathlessly, thinking fast.

The woman picked up the rest of her belongings. "It's okay, nothing's missing."

"I sorry," Alex murmured, hanging his head, and he meant it.

"My dear, the universe is perfect. The rain came to my aid." Her voice had a warm lilt which Alex liked very much.

Suddenly a voice boomed, "YOU! GET AWAY FROM HER! *NOW*!"

The woman swung round, clutching at her breast. "Oh, Rodrigo, you made me jump!" She placed her hand lightly on Alex's shoulder just as he was about to run. "It's okay, this nice young man is my friend, *mi amigo*."

"Friend?" The man glanced sharply from one to the other. "I don't think so. Don't let that innocent face fool you. He's a thief. They usually work in pairs. Come, Señora Chang."

Rodrigo's words stung all the more because Alex hated having to steal. Drop dead, Alex spat back at him silently.

Rodrigo turned and a sudden gust of wind lifted the mop of black shaggy hair pasted onto his scalp. It swirled downwards through the air like a helicopter without propellers. Before it could hit the ground, Señora Chang reached out and grabbed it.

"AH-HA-HA!" Alex roared raucously.

Rodrigo turned purple. "Thank you, Señora Chang," he said stiffly. He plonked the hairpiece back in place and held it there. "Shall we go?" Big drops of rain plopped onto the umbrella.

Señora Chang hesitated. "What's your name?" She smiled down at Alex.

"I am A—" He remembered Rico's warning in the nick of time. "I am Juan."

"Look at his face, he's lying," said Rodrigo smugly, fixing him with a malevolent eye.

The woman ignored him. "And I'm Trixie Chang. Shelter with me at my hotel, Juan. It'll be fun."

Lightning ripped across the sky, followed by deafening thunder. Before they could move, the heavens opened up and rain came pelting down. Without another word, Alex pulled away and sped off towards Plaza de Coral. As he passed an alleyway, someone yanked him by the collar.

"What took you so long? Did you get it?" Rico hissed, pulling him into the shelter of a doorway.

"No, how could I?"

"You could have snatched it while the hotel security was chasing me, and headed off in the other direction, but you blew it."

Alex rounded on him, his eyes spitting fire. "*I* blew it?" he raged. "You almost got caught! I said a storm was coming, but you wouldn't listen!"

"Caught? *Me*? Impossible," his friend drawled airily. "Don't you know nothing ever happens to Rico Marquez?" He pulled out a penknife and started whittling away at the stick he had picked up on the beach. "You are too cautious to be a good thief, *niño*. You will have to do better when we carry out plan B."

"What's plan B?"

Rico shrugged. "I haven't worked it out yet."

Alex stared gloomily out at the slashing rain, shivering periodically. "What's there to work out? Everywhere is closed and there is nobody on the street except us."

"I said today would be a bad day and I was right! What a mess! We could break into the bakery …"

"No! Maria will get into more trouble!"

"Good point. Well, we could … ah …" Rico began to ponder deeply. "Yes, maybe … It could work … but what if …?"

Alex leaned against the wall and waited while Rico argued it out with himself.

"Got it!" said Rico excitedly. "I know a trader who exports tropical birds. He will pay very well for something rare. All we have to do is break into the Paradiso and steal one of the birds."

Alex gawked at him, then started to snigger. "Rico, you're *loco*! We can't sell animals from the zoo."

"Why not? Have you ever been to the zoo, *niño*?"

"No."

"Well I have, and it's filled with the same animals you can find in the forest, so let them catch another one."

"I don't want to do it. I hate stealing. Besides, the zoo is right beside Cree Kee Forest, where Grandfather Talking Dove lives."

The smile faded from Rico's lips. "*Niño*, do you want to find your mother or not?" Alex nodded. "And how do you expect to do it without money? To do anything, you have to have money. If you can't earn enough to get what you want then you have to steal. The police chief steals, the traders steal, the tourists steal, everybody steals. That's reality, so don't get all high and mighty with me. We'll do it and that's that."

Alex opened his mouth to say no again, but something inside stopped him. He averted his eyes sullenly and said no more.

As soon as the rain eased, the two friends set off on foot, being careful to stay off the main roads in town. They walked through Punto Del Cielo to the long road which stretched all the way to the zoo and Cree Kee Forest. Twenty minutes later, they arrived at the Paradiso to find the whole place looking gloomy and deserted. The misty forest loomed behind.

Alex clasped his arms tightly over his chest, while Rico carefully surveyed the sturdy wire mesh fence surrounding the zoo.

"There must be a hole somewhere. All fences have holes in them. You go that way and I will go this way. Keep your eyes off the forest and the forest will keep its eye off of you. Whistle when you find a hole."

"Okay."

It didn't take Alex long to find one right at the back of the zoo, and soon they were prowling past the lions' cage, past the giant armadillos, the butterfly farm, twisting and turning through a maze of animals until—

"What luck! Look!" Alex almost screeched with excitement.

"*Shhhh*, don't stir the animals up," warned Rico.

"I see a fowl with strange feathers."

"Where?"

Alex pointed to an enclosure on his left. Sure enough, there it was, a pale blue and violet fowl scratching around in the dirt. Its feathers shimmered like silk.

"It's a sign," said Rico with a satisfied smile. "It escaped the pen just for us." He dug into his pocket and handed Alex two pieces of twine. "Do exactly as I say."

He hoisted Alex over the limestone wall, then scrambled over himself. Crouching on all fours, he edged forward slowly, calling softly, "cheep, cheep, cheep, cheep." He put his hand in another pocket, found the screwed up wax paper with no more than the smell of the empanada left on it, and held it out to the fowl. Warily the fowl picked its way towards him and when it was close enough, Rico pounced.

"SQUAWK!" The fowl protested.

Rico grabbed its beak and signalled to Alex to wrap the twine around it. "And tie its feet too." Alex did the best he could with the struggling fowl. "Okay, let's go."

They made it back to the hole in record time. Alex went first, then reached in and took the fowl. As Rico was squeezing through the hole, which seemed to have shrunk in his absence, the fowl tried to peck at Alex with its muzzled beak. Instinctively, he held it away from him. It wriggled and fluttered and scratched until Alex could no longer keep a firm grip. Out of his hands it slipped. The twine around its legs unravelled and the fowl scuttled away, fleeing for its life.

"Get it!" hissed Rico, still squirming his way out.

Alex sped after the fowl. It darted this way, then that, leading him on a merry chase. So intent was he on catching it that he did not realize he had entered Cree Kee Forest until he felt a sharp jerk that sent him sprawling.

TALKING DOVE SPEAKS

As ALEX LAY ON THE GROUND, a figure reared up over him, screeching like the blazes, its face contorted. For a moment he thought he saw horns growing out of its skull, but they were toucan feathers. He was staring into the face of the medicine man.

"AYYEEEEE, HUMMPH!" Grandfather Talking Dove yelled, bearing down on him with a stick.

Too late, Alex shut his eyes and tried to play dead. He held his breath and waited.

Above him, the medicine man suddenly became silent. Alex could hear nothing, not a breath. His lungs were at breaking point and still the silence continued, as if the medicine man too was holding his breath.

The next minute, he heard a burst of laughter, and Grandfather Talking Dove began to stamp his feet and his stick in a rhythmic dance. He spun and laughed and stomped and laughed until his rhythm became so infectious, Alex broke into a grin.

"Aha!" Grandfather Talking Dove slapped his own leg gleefully. "I have brought you back to life. Rise up, my son."

"No you didn't," Alex found himself saying, "I was only pretending." He sat up and looked around, catching a glimpse, through the trees, of Grandfather Talking Dove's cabin. "But now I'm going to die for sure," he added gloomily.

"Why so keen to leave Mother Earth?" There was amusement in Grandfather Talking Dove's voice.

"Everyone knows that anyone who looks at you will die, so I don't have a choice, do I?"

The old man let out a cackle, and wrinkles of laughter swallowed up his eyes. "Well, well, well! Do you wish to die?"

"Course not! I'm too young, plus I—" Alex stopped short.

Grandfather Talking Dove nodded sympathetically, as if he already knew what Alex was about to say. He reached into his pocket and pulled out a flat amulet on a leather strap. "Take this, and I will see to it that you come to no harm."

Alex stood up. "You mean if I keep it, I won't die?"

"Not for a long, long time."

Alex took the amulet and turned it over. It was made of a heavy maroon-tinted material, circular, with a dancing figure in the middle. "Thanks." He put it on and tucked it safely under his T-shirt. "But ... why did you kill the other people who looked at you, and you're not going to kill me?"

Grandfather Talking Dove studied him, his expression unreadable. At length he said, "You know, people often come to me when they are already at journey's end."

"I don't understand."

"They were dying before they met me, and I could not help them live. Your journey, however, is about to begin, son of Moon Woman."

Alex's chest tightened until he could hardly breathe. A whisper came out. "You ... you know my mother?"

"I know her very well. I also know of your search for her."

"¡Anda!" Alex suddenly exclaimed, smacking his forehead. "Now I recognise your voice. You were the person outside our cottage whispering about people disappearing!"

Grandfather Talking Dove nodded.

A weight lifted from Alex's shoulders. "You must know where Mami is."

"I don't."

"But Maria said you can see things."

"So can you."

"Not anymore," said Alex despondently.

Grandfather Talking Dove fell silent, thinking. At length, he rose and walked to the centre of the clearing beyond his cabin, beckoning for Alex to follow. Alex obeyed, grabbing up his backpack as he went. He watched the medicine man draw a wide circle around them and light a fire. Unlike the rest of Alma, the ground was remarkably dry.

"Grandfather Talking Dove, why do some wishes come true and not others?"

"As long as they don't interfere with another's destiny, all true wishes come to pass. Some take a moment, others a lifetime. It depends on a person's determination and patience."

The medicine man pulled out a handful of purple dust from a pouch around his waist and threw it into the flames. Purple smoke billowed outwards. He donned a ceremonial poncho and sat down cross-legged.

"There seems to be some kind of shield around Moon Woman, which neither you nor I can penetrate. But perhaps what we cannot do separately we may succeed at together. Come, Alex Springfeather, let us both hold a vision of your mother."

Alex joined him.

After a while, Grandfather Talking Dove began to chant:

"Let the veil of density part,
And Great Spirit enter my heart.
That I may quickly find
What lies in the Cosmic Mind."

As the chanting became more intense, the air grew hot and still, and the purple smoke began to billow upwards in a perfect column. For a split second, Alex felt as if his mother was trying to reach out to him, then the feeling was gone.

Abruptly the chanting stopped, and the smoke hung in mid-air. Grandfather Talking Dove stared into it, his eyes glazed over, until at length the smoke faded away. "Where the feather meets the fox, Moon Woman will dance," he rasped. "The panman will point the way."

"The *panman*?" Alex pulled the silver figurine from his backpack. "How?"

Grandfather Talking Dove said nothing. Except for the distant roar of waterfalls, the forest remained silent too.

Alex placed it on the ground and watched it intently. "It doesn't move."

The silence grew even greater.

"It *can't* move." Disappointed, Alex shoved the panman back into his backpack. "You're making this up. I didn't see or hear anything. I'd be a fool to trust you."

The medicine man bowed humbly. "I am a reflection of your potential, Son of Moon Woman. Trust yourself. Be open to the adventure."

"Adventure?" Alex lashed out. "I don't want to hear that word. 'Our grand adventure begins,' Mami said in Corazon, and looked what happened! Only rich people have adventures. When you have nothing, you have to spend all your time begging and stealing, and people treat you like dirt. That's reality, old man."

"Is it?" Grandfather Talking Dove spoke softly, but his smouldering eyes pierced Alex. He reached for his stick. It snapped off the ground into his hand as if drawn to a magnet. Speechless, Alex watched him leap up and walk a few paces towards the edge of the circle.

Suddenly he whipped round. His swirling poncho fanned the flames. "TELL ME, WHEN A CHILD IS BORN, DOES IT COME OUT OF ITS MOTHER'S WOMB BEGGING? DOES IT GLANCE AROUND SLYLY, PLOTTING HOW TO STEAL FROM OTHERS? HAVE YOU FORGOTTEN YOUR TRUE NATURE, ALEX SPRINGFEATHER?"

His hair streamed behind him, as though a stiff wind was blowing through the forest. The fire spat and crackled. Flames shot out in all directions.

Alex scrabbled up. He looked around for an escape, only to find himself surrounded. A young anteater, two monkeys, a seagull, a mongoose, a doe and her baby, and a huge tortoise, blocked his path. All the animals wore bandages or splints. A high pitched *ahh-iiii!* cut through the air. The blaze in the medicine man's eyes died down and a broad grin spread across his face. He turned to a three-toed sloth with a black eye patch hanging lazily from a tree.

"Ah, Fausto my friend, you're here at last! Come, let us show Alex Springfeather how to enjoy life." He dropped his stick and strode over to the tree. The sloth slipped into his arms. All of a sudden, the medicine man began to stomp and hop around the clearing.

Astounded, Alex jumped out of his way.

"We love, we laugh, we play, we craft, ayyeeeehhh!" Grandfather Talking Dove cried. "We learn, we grow, we flower, we flow, ayyeeeehhh!"

His vitality was infectious. Soon the two monkeys were doing three-legged flips. The mongoose rose on its hind legs and did a lame jig. The seagull careened around the clearing, honking like a runaway bus. The tortoise rocked back and forth, creaking like an old tree.

Before long, Alex too was stomping and grinning. "This is just like a circus!"

Grandfather Talking Dove came to a halt in front of him. "Actually, it's my clinic, and these are my patients." He deposited the sloth in Alex's arms. "Come." Retrieving his medicine bag from the porch, he signalled to Alex to sit. "Watch those claws!" He removed the patch and proceeded to clean the sloth's oozing eye. "Alex Springfeather, if life is not fun, you're not really living. Your mother is gone. I can't change that fact. What I can do is help you fulfil your destiny. Interested?"

"Maybe," Alex muttered, mesmerized by the medicine man's speed. It took just seconds for him to prepare a poultice of crushed roots and paste it over the animal's closed eye.

"Look into Fausto's good eye. What do you see?"

Alex shrugged. "Nothing. Oh, look! I see a tiny me!"

"Uh-huh, and more. Trust. Fausto's trust in you is a reflection of your trust in him. Life is like that, like a mirror. Whatever you send out will come back to you."

"I didn't make anybody's mother disappear, so why did it happen to me?"

"Perhaps Great Spirit wants to teach you a lesson."

"*Me?* But I wasn't that bad," Alex protested hotly, "I know worse children with parents and brothers and sisters and nice houses to live in. Why not teach them a lesson?" He released the sloth and took the seagull from Grandfather Talking Dove.

"That's a good question, the answer for which lies within you."

"Ha! Meaning you don't know."

The medicine man carefully removed the seagull's bandage and examined its wing. "Good. Healed. Off you go." He set the bird on the ground. It flapped its wings and wobbled like a fledgling. "To the outside world you appear young, Alex, yet your spirit is old and wise. But you already know this. You've always listened to your wisdom voice and it has guided you well."

"It stopped working."

"No, it didn't. Despite your fears about me, you found your way here, and now you're one step closer to finding your mother."

"Am I?" Alex eyed him doubtfully. "But I don't understand the message. I don't know what to do next."

The young anteater shuffled up, its droopy snout weighed down by a leafy pack. "It takes courage to move forward when the future is unclear." Grandfather Talking Dove removed the pack and began to redress the wound made by a big cat's claw. "Yanye here can attest to that. He's an orphan, and the gutsiest anteater I know." Finished, he slapped his knees and rose. "Well, son of Moon Woman, time for you to rejoin your friend."

"Rico! I forgot about him!" Alex sprang up.

"Wait." Grandfather Talking Dove hurried into the cabin and came back out with a bag. "Take this."

Alex opened it and the sweet aroma of food assailed him. "Empanadas, and roasted corn, and arepas!"

"And I have something else for you." The medicine man went around the side of the cabin and brought back a fowl with shimmering blue and violet feathers.

"You caught it!" Alex's face fell. "We— we stole it from the zoo to sell it, but I suppose you want us to take it back."

"No, not this one. The one you took from the zoo has been given its freedom. This one has agreed to be imprisoned in a cage so you may have the money to do what you want to do."

"H-he *agreed*? Did he speak to you, d-do birds speak to you?" Alex stammered.

"Birds, dogs, trees, everything has a voice, if you listen. We've been friends for about ... eight months, eh?" Grandfather Talking Dove stroked the bird gently, and the bird replied with a low clucking sound. "Take him, he won't give you any trouble."

"Thanks, Grandfather Talking Dove," said Alex earnestly. "You saved my skin. Will I see you again?"

"Come and visit anytime you wish."

"But how will I find you? I don't even know where I am."

"You will." Grandfather Talking Dove walked him to the edge of the clearing and pointed. "Just keep walking that way, and in no time at all you'll be back where you started."

Alex set off through the trees with a backward wave. For the first time in weeks, his heart felt light. Moments later, he had the strangest sensation of being in two places at the same time. Next thing he knew, he was outside the forest watching Rico heave himself out of the hole with great difficulty.

Clutching the bird and the bag of food, he ran towards his friend, shouting, "Rico! Rico! You'll never guess what happened!"

"You caught it! Good!" Rico bounded up to him and took the fowl. "I thought it would vanish into the forest and we would have to say bye-bye to dinner and bus fare."

"It did! This is a different one!" Alex exclaimed. "But what happened to you, did you get stuck in the fence? I was gone for ages."

Rico snickered. "No, I did not get stuck in the fence. Hunger must be gnawing at your brain for a few seconds to turn into ages."

"But I was in the forest for a long time with Grandfather Talking Dove."

"*You* were in Cree Kee Forest with the medicine man?" Disbelief blazed in Rico's eyes. "You're lying."

"I'm not," Alex replied indignantly. "Our fowl ran into the forest and disappeared. Grandfather Talking Dove said it was given its freedom, and he gave me this one instead. He said—"

Rico let out a shriek and dropped the fowl. It flopped on its side and lay between them fluttering slightly. It uttered not a sound. "You really saw the medicine man?" he gasped.

"Uh-huh."

"What does he look like?"

"He's tall and thin, and has long, long, hair with toucan feathers sticking out. His face is as wrinkled as a raisin. Sometimes his eyes are scary, but he has a nice smile."

"Alex, my brother, you're a dead duck," Rico wailed.

"No I'm not. He said no harm will come to me."

And Alex told Rico most of what transpired in Cree Kee Forest. When he was finished, Rico chuckled. "So tell me, while you were sniffing purple dust, did time wait for you?"

"That's the thing I don't understand. Maybe when I went into Cree Kee Forest, I went into a different time. When I was coming back, I just went like *wsshhh!* and I was back where I started, just like the old man said! I think he can split time."

"What a load of goat dung! *Split* time? I never heard of such a thing! You never saw the medicine man."

"You think so? Well tell me how I got this then!" Alex opened the bag of food and shoved it under Rico's nose. "And *this*?" He pulled out the amulet.

"*Madre de dios,* the Mystic's Amulet!" Rico backed away in dread. "You're cursed! I shouldn't have brought you here." Scratching his head, he scuttled around in a circle frantically muttering, "What shall I do, what shall I do?" until Alex grew quite giddy.

"Stop Rico, please!" he begged. "Grandfather Talking Dove said the amulet will keep me safe. He knows my mother. They're good friends. He's from our clan."

Rico stopped. "Good friends?" he repeated stupidly. "He and Tia Lucia?"

Alex nodded vigorously. "He came to my house the day she disappeared, but I didn't know it was him."

Rico eyed him hesitantly. "Well ... maybe he doesn't kill people. Maybe that's old men's tales, like Maria said, but I don't like the sound of him." He picked up the bird. "Give me the bag, and you hold the bird." They exchanged, and Rico took out a patty and bit into it. "Mmm, he can cook! But a person who can change time is not to be trusted. Tia Lucia keeps dangerous friends. What did he mean, she'll be dancing where the feather meets the fox? Are we supposed to look for a place with that name? Is your mother a nightclub hostess?"

"No. I told you she's a healer."

"And how is the panman supposed to point the way? It's just a clump of metal."

"I know."

"Crazy old man," Rico muttered under his breath. "Let's go."

"Where?"

"To sell the bird. We can be out of here this very afternoon and on our way to a new town."

Alex stared at the docile creature in his arms, then suddenly tossed it back in the direction of Cree Kee Forest. "Run!"

He waited for the bird to disappear behind some bushes before turning to face his friend.

Rico was so taken aback he could not speak for a moment. In any case, his mouth was full. Flakes of pastry fell from his lips as he gaped at the disappearing bird. "Thash it, I'm done wish you," he finally spluttered, spewing bits of food everywhere. "You're inshane." Clutching the bag of food to his chest, he stormed off.

Alex caught up with him on the road back to Punto del Cielo. "I had to do it, Rico. The bird is Grandfather Talking Dove's friend. He gave us his *friend*! How could I put his friend in a cage?"

Rico ignored him.

"We'll find a better way to make money, believe me."

"How?"

"By wishing for it."

"Right. We'll just say, I wish, and money will fall from the sky."

"Come on, Rico, don't be mad. If I'm wrong, I'll give you ... I'll give you my whale and dolphin T-shirt."

"I wouldn't be seen dead in that girly shirt," Rico growled. He stuck the bag of food in Alex's hand. "Here, take one. Only one! This food must last until you make us some money." Alex grinned. Rico couldn't stay angry for long. "And let's hope we don't meet anyone we don't want to meet before we do."

But they did meet someone they would have preferred not to meet. As soon as they reached the old part of town, they smelled the moth-eaten black suit long before they reached the alley in which Rojo the Rake Thief was lurking. The person he was conversing with nipped into a doorway out of sight.

"*Hermanos*," Rojo simpered as they passed by. "Surely you can spare a patty or two."

"After you stole from us? You have nerve," said Rico, pausing.

"It wasn't me," Rojo whined, his eyes darting here and there shiftily. "Just a little bun? I'm hungry."

The moment Alex opened the bag, Rojo stuck his hand in and picked out an arepa stuffed with cheese and meat. He gobbled it down and stretched out his hand for more.

"*¡Basta!*" said Rico, taking the bag from Alex. "Let's go."

Rojo's bushy brows shot together in a straight line menacingly. "If you don't give me another one, I'll tell the police you stole from the bakery."

"Ah, go on your way, Rojo!" said Rico impatiently. As he and Alex walked away, he added under his breath, *"Burrico."*

Rojo's lips curled into a sinister sneer. "We shall soon see who is the ass."

THE PERFECT SOLUTION

Punto del Cielo was a dreary place without the loggers and miners. The grubby beer gardens and seedy eating houses were as quiet as tombs. Piles of sodden rubbish lay in alleyways where cheerful higglers once parked themselves. Hungry stray dogs roamed the streets. Hurrying to get out of the area, Alex and Rico took a shortcut down a narrow, potholed lane. Up ahead, a burly blond man in a red alligator jacket and matching cowboy boots was squinting at the street sign.

"Hoy! What's that I see?" Rico exclaimed. "A worm out of his hole! You see, *niño*? It's not always the early bird that catches the worm. Watch this." He handed the bag of food to Alex and sidled up to the man. "Can I help you, Mister?" His voice oozed friendliness.

The man swivelled around slowly and tried to focus on Rico's face. "Dang wind keesh blowun' the shign," he muttered, swaying. "Can't shee a dang theng!"

"What's he saying?" Alex whispered, coming up behind Rico.

"He says the wind is blowing the sign, and he can't see it." Alex snickered and Rico's eyes gleamed. "He's drunk as a skunk." He placed a hand on the man's broad shoulder. "You want to go to Plaza de Coral, buddee?"

"*Shee, shee, Ameego*!" Spittle flew everywhere. "Whish way'zat?" The man staggered around in a confused circle.

"Don't worry, I will take you, okay?"

Relief flooded the man's face. "Good boy!"

A cunning look appeared on Rico's features. "But you pay me first, okay buddee?"

"Okay, *Ameego*."

"And my friend too." Rico winked at Alex.

"Deal!" The man lurched forward to shake Rico's hand. "Name'sh Rick, whash yoursh?"

"*Rick*?" Rico stole a glance at Alex. "Is a lucky name! I am Carlos, and this is Juan," he lied with a straight face.

Rick beamed. "Hey."

He chucked Alex playfully under the chin, almost knocking him off his feet. Then he reached round for his back pocket and slowly coaxed his snakeskin wallet out. Nudging each other, Rico and Alex waited expectantly.

"How'zish?" Rick flashed four brand new bills before their noses.

Rico snatched the bills and stuffed them swiftly into his pocket. "His eyes are so crossed, he gave us eighty American dollars!" he hissed excitedly to Alex. "We're rich! I knew it, I knew we'd make a load today!"

"You did not!" Alex hissed back, bursting with excitement. "*I* told you if we wish for it, it would come."

Grinning sloppily at them, Rick reached behind. He shoved the wallet down with a flourish, and missed his rear pants pocket. When it hit the ground, Rico took one look at it, glanced at Rick, hesitated for an instant, then scooped it up. He wiggled the wallet playfully in the man's face. Grinning idiotically, the man tried to get it back. He reeled back and forth like a wobbly top on a string.

Alex started laughing and couldn't stop. He laughed so hard, his sides began to ache. "Stop, Rico," he finally gasped, "you're killing me!"

Rico snapped round. Alex clapped a hand to his mouth and stared back at Rico in horror. His name had just slipped right out. Seizing the opportunity, Rick snatched his wallet back. Furious, Rico grappled with him and the wallet fell again. He lunged just as Rick bent down to retrieve it. Their heads collided with a resounding THWACK! Rick went down like a log. His head made an awful sound when it hit the ground.

A somewhat dazed Rico stood over the prostrate figure rubbing his forehead and grimacing with pain.

"WHAT DID YOU DO THAT FOR?" Alex shrieked.

Tentatively, Rico knelt beside Rick and prodded him. Except for the slight rise and fall of his chest, the man showed no sign of life. Alex poked him timidly on the cheek with a frayed sneaker toe. Blood began to seep from under his head. Petrified, they watched the horrific expanding blob as it slowly gobbled up the pebbles on the gravel road. Out of the corner of his eye, Alex saw movement. He glanced over his shoulder at the abandoned building behind.

"Someone is watching."

"Let's get out of here," said Rico roughly, trying to hide the tremor in his voice.

"But we have to do something."

"No we don't. Move it!" Rico ordered. With Rick's wallet clutched in his hand, he ran like the blazes towards the town centre. Alex followed.

"Drop it, Rico, drop it!"

"What for?" Rico yelled back, dodging through an alley and nipping across the old timber yard.

"Well ... at least ... let's ... tell ... someone!" Alex wheezed.

Rico slowed to a trot.

"ARE YOU *LOCO?*" he bawled when Alex caught up with him. "Nobody will believe it was an accident! Anyway, he shouldn't have strayed off the tourist beat. They tell all the tourists to stay away from the old part of town. Let's go."

Eventually they stopped in the side street behind the bakery. Rico opened the wallet and counted the bills. His eyes bulged. "*Niño*, we are beyond rich! We could go to the end of the earth with this!"

Alex shook his head adamantly. "It's wrong, Rico, to take someone's money and leave them dying. I have a bad feeling."

"Don't say that, you're going to jinx us!" Rico put an arm around him. "Look, I feel bad about the worm too, but really, the accident happened for the best. He'll recover, and learn next time to stay out of trouble. We get to search every town until we find your mother. What could be wrong about that? Come on, let's board the first bus out of here."

Dragging his feet, Alex went with him. At the bus terminal, they walked up and down, checking the destination of each bus, but he didn't feel inclined to get on any of them.

Rico finally confronted him. "What do you mean they're all going the wrong way?" he said impatiently. "How would you know which way is right?"

Alex's eyes strayed over his shoulder. *"Policia,* Rico! RUN!"

An enormous paw landed on Rico's shoulder. He tried to duck away. The policeman grabbed his arm in a vice grip.

"Save yourself!" Rico shouted.

Alex dropped the bag of food and kicked Rico's captor on the shin with all his might. Rico shook loose from the howling officer, and they plunged into the crowd.

"We have to split up," Rico hissed, glancing back. "There are at least four flies on our tail. Go to Carpo The Butcher. I'll meet you there as soon as I can!"

Crouching low, he scuttled away, heading towards the river that wound through the cocoa plantations. Alex, instead of going to Carpo, fled back the way they came. He didn't stop running until he barrelled into Grandfather Talking Dove, who seemed to be waiting at the edge of Cree Kee Forest. The medicine man took Alex not to his cabin, but to another spot no more than a hundred paces into the forest.

"Welcome to my evening retreat," he said with a twinkle in his eye.

They were in a smaller clearing with nothing but a simple hammock strung between two trees. It felt airy and cool here. Alex shrugged his backpack off, and tumbled into the hammock. Sweat poured off his trembling body.

"Do you think Rico is safe too?" he panted worriedly, after he recounted what happened.

"Hush, now," said Grandfather Talking Dove gently, "let mind follow body."

He busied himself with the task of building a fire.

Alex closed his eyes and fell into a fitful sleep.

Mami … Don't go!

Alex awoke with a start. Looking around confused, his eyes fell on his backpack. It was open. The snaps had come loose. He knew without having to check.

"My panman! It's gone!" he howled, rolling out of the hammock.

"Go look for it," said Grandfather Talking Dove coolly. He was relaxing against a log.

Alex moved towards him, pleading. "The police are after me. Can't you search for me?"

"What you start, you must finish."

"Fine, don't help! See if I care!"

Alex ran through the trees, retracing his steps. He jogged down the long road in the dimming light, scanning the ground as he went. All of a sudden the wind was knocked out of him. He flipped through the air and landed in a crumpled heap on a mound of sand.

71

A tall man rushed to his aid. "You okay, son?"

Alex gazed at him blankly.

"Can you speak?" A woman took his hand anxiously. Her face was familiar. "I'm sorry, I didn't see you coming. I bent down to pick up—"

Suddenly a shadow appeared beside them and scooped Alex up in its arms. "Come with me … and bring that," said Grandfather Talking Dove briskly.

"But our bikes …" the woman protested weakly.

A pair of rented scooters sat outside the zoo's gate.

"Leave them, they'll be safe."

He strode into the forest. Intrigued, the couple followed.

Grandfather Talking Dove deposited the dazed Alex in the hammock, and invited the couple to join him around the fire. Seated, the woman unwrapped the bundle she found on the road. "Such detail! It's exquisite." She turned it over. *Plonk, plonk, plink, plonk,* it went.

Alex shot up. "My panman! You found it!" He hopped out of the hammock, took it from her and clasped it tightly to his chest. "Thank you, Señora Trixie Chang! I— it— Mami— " He bit his lip, fighting the tears of relief.

"There, there, my dear." Trixie Chang gathered him in her arms. Over his head, she looked enquiringly at Grandfather Talking Dove.

"It's the end of tough day for him."

Over cups of bush tea, Grandfather Talking Dove shared Alex's tale with the Changs.

"I want to help him," said Trixie Chang determinedly. "This silver panman that means so much to him, brought us together for a reason, I know it." She shot a glance at her husband. "Francis told me to leave the bundle alone, but I had the strangest sense that I should pick it up."

Francis Chang ruffled Alex's hair. "And you were right, Trixie." He turned to the medicine man. "We work for an international aid organization. I fly around the area frequently delivering supplies to villages. I'd be happy to make enquiries about his mother. Meanwhile, he can come back to Awara and stay with us for as long as he likes."

"Sounds like the perfect solution." Grandfather Talking Dove stoked the fire. "What do you think, Alex Springfeather?"

"I want to go with them. Señora Chang has eyes like Mami," murmured Alex drowsily, his head propped against her shoulder. "Plus my Grandpapi was born in Awara. I want to see what it looks like. After I find Mami, we'll go back to our cottage on Señora Lagrima's hacienda."

"Son, it may take a while to settle the good Señora's affairs," said Grandfather Talking Dove ruefully. "Her relatives are squabbling over the property, so a judge will have to decide."

Alex frowned briefly. "You said all true wishes come to pass, right?" The medicine man nodded. "Then the judge will give us our cottage."

"How well we speak English now," Trixie murmured. "You know, I would have been happy to give you boys that little radio, if you had asked."

Alex went hot with shame. He turned away and pretended to rub his eye.

She pulled his face towards her. "You wouldn't ever try to con me again, I hope."

He shook his head vigorously. "Oh no, Señora, never ever."

"Good." She touched his cheek lightly.

"Well that settles it. Tomorrow, we'll begin making plans for your trip." Francis Chang stretched out his long legs and leaned back against the log contentedly.

"It looks like that panman of yours has begun to move, Son of Moon Woman!" Grandfather Talking Dove winked at Alex.

"You're coming too, right?"

"And leave my forest friends? No, son, you must go alone. It's *your* adventure."

"Alone!" Alex jerked upright, fully awake. "Rico! I have to find him! We were supposed to meet at Carpo The Butcher, but I don't think he's there. Something's wrong!"

"You sensed right. He got caught. He's now in jail."

Alex gaped at the medicine man momentarily, then anger filled him. "Stupid, stupid Rico!" he cried, pounding the dirt with his fist. "I said I had a bad feeling, but he wouldn't listen." A dread gripped him. "Do— do you know what happened to the man?"

"He's in hospital with a very bad concussion."

Alex bit his lip. "I have to stay and help Rico."

"If you really want to help him, you'll let him follow the path of his own making. You must go where the panman leads you, and that's to Awara with the Changs."

THE SEARCH FOR THE
FEATHER AND THE FOX

THE CHANG HOUSEHOLD AT 281 OLEANDER DRIVE was far from orderly. Sita, the scatterbrained housekeeper, left dishrags in the freezer and brooms in the trees. Yaso, the Changs' adopted daughter, put drummer roaches in Sita's hair and tied her skirt to the kitchen table while she baked. Trixie and Francis worked out of a little studio attached to the house.

A freshly painted sign above the door said, CANIDO INTERNATIONAL AID ORGANIZATION. There was just enough space between the boxes of supplies to reach the phone when it rang, and no space at all to sit. The office chairs were under the flamboyant tree.

When Alex arrived, he and Yaso hit it off right away, becoming partners-in-crime. Upon hearing of the search for Tia Lucia, Yaso announced to her parents over their first dinner together, "Alex and me going be the sleuces and you can help us."

"Sleuths. But shouldn't it be the other way round?" asked Trixie mildly. "After all, we're the ones with the means to travel to surrounding villages."

"But Tia Lucia not in surrounding village, she *here*. That's why the panman want to come," Yaso argued matter-of-factly. "And who know here better than me? Not you two. You don't go nowhere 'cept work."

"Well then," said Francis, with a twinkle in his eye, "Upper Awara is all yours. We'll take the lower end, and the rest of the planet."

Yaso scowled at him. She knew fully well what that meant: they were being restricted to the neighbourhood.

Alex felt a growing excitement. Already he loved this town where his Papi's family came from. He had a panoramic view from his bedroom window. Arrays of houses clung to the hillside below. Their red, green and blue corrugated zinc roofs shimmered in the heat. All the backyards were full of fruit trees, just like the yard in which he grew up. There was a forest nearby too, and a red water creek at the foot of the hill. The bedroom itself was spacious and had a wall unit that suited him perfectly. On the first shelf, he put shells and a bottle of sand from around his old cabana, and some rocks from Cree Kee Forest. On the very top, he placed the silver panman and the Mystic's Amulet.

The next day, he and Yaso settled down under the star-apple tree in the backyard to work out a plan.

Clue #1: Where the feather meets the fox, Moon Woman dance, Yaso wrote faithfully in her notebook. She eyed Alex thoughtfully, squinting from time to time and tugging at her stubby pigtails. Eventually she said,
"I getting a feeling … Yeh! Let's go!"

"Where?"

"To search the Hindu Mandir. It have animal pictures, and at Phagwah and Divali festivals, people dance."

Down to the simple ginger and white temple they went. Jhandi flags flapped gaily in the breeze at the entrance. They trotted around the outside of the circular building, peering through the open windows. There were many beautiful paintings on the walls, but none of feathers or foxes.

"Hmmm, not here." Yaso paused for a moment beneath a window. "Maybe is a petroglitch!"

"What?"

"Petro-*glyph*. Old rock carving, like the ones behind the benab." Startled, Yaso and Alex looked up. A man in white leaned through the window with an affectionate grin on his face. "What scampishness you planning now, eh Yaso?"

"Pandit Sharma," said Yaso guiltily, "I din't see you! We looking for a feather and a fox to solve a numdrum."

"Conundrum."

"Uh-huh. This is Alex. He just come across the borderline to live with us."

"Ahhh! Enjoying yourself, Alex?"

Alex nodded vigorously.

"Good. You might find what you want uphill. If not— " he glanced around furtively and then whispered, "I hear people say a magic fox lives in Towa-Towa Forest. It flies, so perhaps it has feathers."

"We looking for something real," said Yaso, rolling her eyes. "That's a Nansi story, Pandit Sharma."

"You never know." With a wave, Pandit Sharma disappeared from the window.

Yaso dragged Alex out into the road. "I tell a lie to fool him," she whispered gleefully. "The fox real, but it don't want people to know."

Alex gasped. "You *saw* it? A flying fox with feathers?"

"It don't have feathers, at least I don't think so. I din't see it for real yet … I only see it in a dream."

Perplexed, Alex watched as Yaso opened her notebook and wrote, Clue #2: magic fox in Towa-Towa Forest.

"C'mon, let's go!"

Uphill they climbed to the benab. Under the palm-thatched roof of the hut, Amerindian artisans were crafting ornaments, hammocks, clothing and many other beautiful things. Two young people were giggling and dancing around the wallaba posts. Alex felt a surge of excitement. Behind the benab was a wall of stone, and behind that, a miniature waterfall and pool. Alex and Yaso carefully examined the carvings on the surrounding rocks. They saw fish, and tapir and a macaw perched on a limb, but no fox.

Alex tried to hide his disappointment. An artisan saw the glumness in his face as he passed back, and gave him a tiny anteater made of balata. It reminded him of Yanye, the orphan anteater in Cree Kee Forest, and it cheered him up.

Yaso stopped just beyond the benab and wrote, Clue #3: Macaw on branch.

"Why? Why is that a clue?"

"It has feathers, don't it?"

"But we're looking for a fox and a feather together," said Alex, exasperated. "They have to meet!"

"I know what I doing."

Alex sighed.

On the way back down the hill, they spotted a donkey tethered to a post.

"Let's ride it!" he suggested.

They untied it and Alex clambered on.

"Me next!" cried Yaso, tapping the donkey's hind with a stick.

Bucking, the donkey took off. It charged across the road straight into the Sacred Heart Church. Two elders collared Alex as he tried to slither off at the altar and escape. Yaso came tumbling up the aisle and got caught too.

The men led them back to 281 Oleander Drive. Only Sita was home. A CANIDO worker was asleep under the cashew tree. Yaso and Alex breathed a sigh of relief.

"Nah fuss, Dr. Mashado," said Sita, when the shorter of the two elders complained. "Nothing wrong with donkey an' chil'ren attending church."

Frustrated, the two men left.

Sita shooed Alex and Yaso into the kitchen. "Time for coconut ice cream an' jell-O," she squeaked cheerfully.

Just as they were settling down to stuff their faces, she added in a whisper, "By the way, when you do bad, be ready to duck, 'cause it gon come right back like a boomerang."

Alex and Yaso stared at her in alarm. Sita's voice was mousy to begin with. When she whispered, her mouth twisted in all directions and barely a sound came out. She flashed them a broad smile and waddled away. The food did not taste as appetizing after that. They ate quickly and went back to plotting and planning.

For weeks they searched. In Towa-Towa Forest, they found feathers of all sizes and shapes and lots of birds to match, but no magic fox. They combed the streets of Upper Awara, questioning everyone they met. Yaso added more clues to her book. Still they were no closer to solving the riddle of Tia Lucia's whereabouts. Trixie and Francis were having no better luck.

By the beginning of the fifth week, Alex was in a low mood. He lost interest in the search, and took to staring into space for long periods of time.

"It's hard to keep the faith, isn't it?" said Trixie softly, coming up behind him. Alex had been staring out the window at a cat prowling around in the dark. The cat froze near the unlit streetlight across the road and looked up. A shadowy figure slipped from behind the post and walked away quickly. Alex frowned. The slinking gait reminded him of someone.

Trixie put an arm around him. "Whatever happens, you have a home here with us. You know that, don't you?"

Alex started to nod and stopped. Instead, he pulled away. "I have my own home," he said tightly.

Francis looked up from his book. He was sitting in his favourite basket chair under the lamp. "I guess we all need a treat. How about a trip to the savannahs?"

"In the plane?" asked Alex grumpily, but there was a spark of interest in his eyes.

Francis nodded.

"But if we land, we gon' crash into the anthills that tall like you," said Yaso, frowning. She was on the floor pasting pictures into her scrapbook.

Francis roared with laughter and his eyes disappeared into half-moons. "As far as I know, the ants haven't taken over the entire savannah yet. We can leave early Friday morning, overnight at the guest house beside Green Water Creek and return Saturday evening."

"Wish I could come." Trixie flopped into the settee.

"Why not? What do we have assistants for if we can't take a break now and then?"

"Getting the books from the coast to the Moka Library by Friday noon is going to be tricky. Then we have to set them up." She shook her head.

"Too bad."

That night, Alex saw the panman dance in a dream. He was playing a soca tune on the pan and sashaying across a field towards a group of people. Alex could not see their faces. There was too much light. Suddenly the music became discordant, a dull, tinny sound. Alex awoke to find the sun streaming in.

Pang! Pang! Pang! he heard. He tumbled out of bed and rushed to the window. It was only a vendor banging a tin can on the side of his donkey cart.

"GRAPEFRUIT!" the man called in a coarse voice. "SWEET, SWEET ORANGE!"

Alex walked over to the shelf and looked up at the silver panman. For a split second, the panman's face came alive and it winked. Startled, Alex stepped back and tripped over a stool.

"Everything all right?" Trixie called out.

He opened his bedroom door a crack and peered out. She was fluffing her pillows in the master bedroom across the hall. "A cartman woke me up."

"That's Ten Dolla. You'll get used to him. Normally he takes Dury Lane down to the market on the waterfront, but whenever he has extras to sell, he comes around here making a racket. He's a strange bird. Drinks like a fish. Slinks around in the middle of the night. You don't want to have any dealings with him."

Alex nodded and yawned. Closing the door, he rushed back to the shelf. Fixing his gaze on the panman, he waited eagerly. Several minutes passed and nothing happened. Disappointed, he climbed back into bed.

For the next two days, it rained.

On Thursday, Trixie came home from the coast looking soggy. Alex, Yaso and Sita's young godson, Madou, were sitting on the tibisiri mat in the living room playing snakes and ladders.

"I winning, Miss Trixie!" said Madou, his cherubic features alight. Alex and Yaso did not seem enthusiastic.

"Boring day?" asked Trixie lightly.

"It was okay," mumbled Yaso.

Alex nodded, and the two of them beat a hasty retreat out the front door, leaving Madou gaping.

Trixie watched them disappear with a puzzled frown on her face. Entering the dining room, she immediately noticed something odd. The table and chairs had been shifted. "Afternoon, Sita!" she called, dropping her things on the table.

Sita's head popped round the kitchen door. "'Af'noon, Miss Trixie."

Trixie pulled one of the chairs from against the wall. Two legs fell off.

"What the—?" She looked at Sita. Sita was staring at the legs open-mouthed. Trixie laid the chair down, and tried the one next to it. One leg fell off.

Sita began to laugh. "Them chil'ren sneaky, boy! I left them playing, an' went up the road to collect Dou-Dou. Them never say a word when I come back."

"It's not a joke," said Trixie sternly. "Someone could have been hurt."

Sita sobered up immediately. "You right, Miss Trixie. But everybody fine, an' the chairs can fix. Plus you still got four left, so no need to fret."

"Easy for you to say. They're not your children or your dining set."

Trixie turned and marched upstairs to take a long shower.

Dinner that night was a nervous affair. Few words were spoken besides, "Pass the pepperpot, please," and "Eat your greens."

When the meal was over, Trixie cleared her throat. It sounded ominous. "Well, I'm waiting."

The words tumbled out of Alex's mouth. "We didn't expect the legs to fall off. We were practicing breaking boards like the Shaolin monks, and— and—"

"—and you used the chair legs to support the boards," Francis finished up with a half smile. He did not seem angry at all.

Alex and Yaso nodded gratefully. Their eyes swung towards Trixie anxiously.

"Well, Yaso," said Trixie mildly, "let's say some young monks from your Himalayan village did what you did and instead of confessing, they tried to hide the evidence because they were afraid they wouldn't get to attend the next day's festivities. What do you suppose the Lama would do?"

Yaso shifted uneasily. "He would forgive them, 'cause they din't mean bad?" she said hopefully.

"I'm sure he would. I would." Yaso shot Alex a relieved glance. "But I'm also sure he would do what I'm about to do. My dears, consider yourselves apprenticed to the carpenter. Tomorrow, you won't be going anywhere. You'll be learning from him how to mend broken chairs."

"Not fair!" Yaso roared in protest. "We ducked. Bad not s'pose to hit us back!"

"What?"

"Can't you punish us after we go to the Savannahs?" Alex begged.

Francis rose from the table. "The next time, I suggest you do the simplest thing. Take responsibility for your actions."

It was agony watching him toss his bags into the old land cruiser next morning. Trixie was already gone. Before taking off, Francis called Sita outside. Yaso and Alex ran out the backdoor and around to the side of the house to eavesdrop.

"… Yes, I know I gotta stay overnight," Sita was saying. "Madou gon stay too. His mammy going up-creek."

"Good. Now listen, Sita, the children are grounded, which means they're not to leave the yard. I don't want to hear about donkeys on altars or any such escapades when I get back."

Sita's mouth fell open. "How you know 'bout that?"

"That's not important. All I'm saying is, keep your hands on the controls. We're depending on you."

Francis hopped into the land cruiser and left without a backward glance.

Flustered, Sita hustled back to clear the dining table. The room was empty. "Where them chil'ren gone?" She rolled her hair into a bun and stuck a fork in it. "Yaso …? Alex …?" She stepped outside and grabbed the megaphone hanging beside the backdoor. "YASO! ALEX!"

"What?" they chorused, coming out from behind the breadfruit tree by the side of the house.

Sita breathed a visible sigh of relief. "Y'all gotta stay in the yard. You grounded."

"We know," said Yaso sulkily.

The carpenter came and showed Alex and Yaso what to do. By midday, the chairs were like new again. After lunch, Alex lay down in the hammock under the sapodilla tree in a grumpy mood. Yaso plonked herself on the ground beside him.

"I GOING UP THE ROAD TO COLLECT DOU-DOU," Sita called to them from the backdoor. "DON'T MOVE."

Yaso gazed after her with a broad grin. "Sita going out with a fork in her hair, and her apron tie on back to front. I think she having a nervous break-up."

"I don't care."

"Okay." Yaso drew out her notebook. "I getting a next feeling."

"Keep it to yourself."

"You don't wanna know?"

"Not interested."

Yaso looked hurt. "Why you mad at me?"

"Because you don't get it!" Alex shouted. "We'll never find Mami wandering around the streets following your stupid feelings!"

Yaso's mouth fell open in shock and disbelief. "Drone!" she lashed out, jumping up. "I never helping you again!"

"Good!"

Yaso stormed off.

"She doesn't understand!" he muttered, furious at himself and her.

Time was running out. His birthday was in two days. What if he did die? Who would rescue Mami? Alex stared into space, his brows knitted with worry.

Madou came charging up. His brown skin glistened with sweat from running all the way up Oleander Drive. "I wanna play cricket!"

"I'm busy," Alex growled.

"But, I wanna play now."

"I said no! Buzz off!"

Madou tugged at Alex's arm. "C'mon."

Grimly, Alex rose and made a beeline for the coconut tree. Yanking off a piece of a nest, he marched back to Madou and stuffed it down his back. Then he flopped back into the hammock.

Madou wiggled and twisted. "AUNTIE SITA, 'LEX PUT WOOD ANTS ON ME!" he howled, dashing for the house.

Yaso came out. Quickly she helped Madou get his shirt off and dusted him down. "DOUBLE DRONE!" she yelled at Alex, furious. "YOU BETTER DUCK!"

Alex barely heard her. His mind was miles away. Above his head, wild parrots fought over a juicy sapodilla. It dropped on his arm with a splat. Mechanically, he flicked it off. *Papi, I wish you were here to tell me what to do!*

Closing his eyes, he chanted over and over, "I will live, I will find the panman, I will find Mami."

Plonk, plonk, plink, plonk. Opening his eyes, Alex saw

the panman standing on the ground, smiling up at him. Sitting up, he glanced around. There were trees everywhere. Tall trees. The sun had disappeared, but it was not quite night.

"How could this be?" he muttered, climbing out of the hammock. "I was in the backyard, and now I'm in a forest."

The panman raised his hand stiffly and signalled to Alex to follow. He moved so swiftly, Alex had trouble keeping up. Through the forest they ran, until they came to a clearing. A three-storied building loomed. It was surrounded by high walls.

"Where are we?" he asked the panman, but the panman was gone.

Alex walked up to the huge iron gate and tried it. It was locked. He peered inside the compound. It was empty.

"Psssst!"

Alex glanced up. A figure waved frantically at him from a barred window.

Suddenly a voice rasped in his ear. "Thank your lucky stars! You could be there too!"

Alex turned sharply, and came nose to nose with a horrible spectre.

"¡Aiiii!"

"Shhhh! It's me!"

"Mother Hen! I thought you were a ghost! What are you doing here?"

Maria was in white, as usual. This time a hood hid her face. She pulled Alex away from the gate.

"I came to warn you, my little chick," she whispered. "If Rojo The Rake Thief had not seen what happened in Punto del Cielo and turned you boys in, this—"

Alex exploded. *"Rojo* did that? That— that mangy—"

"Now, now," Maria patted him, "he did you a good turn. Better for you not to mix with the likes of Rico, anyway. Look at him."

Alex squinted up at the window. It was indeed Rico, but he could barely recognize him. His face was haggard, his hair was a tangled mess and his eyes were as wild as a cornered beast. The fingers that gripped the window bars were bleeding.

"Dangerous business he's got himself into. I think they mean to kill him."

Alex gasped. "Who? The police?"

"Police?" Maria sniffed. "Who said anything about police? That's a child smugglers' den. The man Rico knocked down is one of them. They believe Rico tried to kill him."

"But it was an accident!" Alex grabbed her. "We have to save him!"

Maria cupped his face in her hands. "Believe me, my little chick, it's too late. Only a change of heart can save Rico now."

"Help me *niño*, help me!" Rico called hoarsely.

"I have to try!"

Alex rattled the gate loudly.

A guard stepped out of a hut nearby. "What's this? Why are you making such a ruckus?"

"It's all a mistake," said Alex frantically. "Rico doesn't belong in there. Free him, please!"

"We don't let people out, we only put people in, and you're next." The guard advanced menacingly.

Charging forward, Alex ploughed into him, taking him by surprise.

"Umph!" The guard fell to his knees.

Quickly, Alex seized a bunch of keys from a hook on his belt and ran for the gate. There was no keyhole or padlock.

"Use your mind!"

Slowly, Alex turned around. The man standing before him winked, and the silver panman he was holding in the crook of one arm winked too. His hair was curlier than Alex's but just as wild, and he had bat ears too. "Papi, you came!" Alex dropped the keys and threw his arms around his father. His father held him tightly.

"Hurry!" Rico pleaded faintly. Other faces appeared in the window behind him.

"You can do it, Alex Springfeather. Don't give up," said Papi, stroking his hair. "Do this, and you'll find the answer to many questions."

The sound of a whistle pierced the air. There was a stampede of feet. Guards were coming from all directions. Alex caught a glimpse of Agouti tattoos on some of their arms. Panicking, he rushed back to the gate and tried to use his mind, but his mind was a jumble.

"Papi!"

Papi and the panman were gone. The Agouti guards surrounded Alex.

"Kill him. Kill the troublemaker. Kill him," they rumbled, their eyes filled with hatred.

"HELP!" Alex cried. In desperation, he plunged into the crowd of guards and tried to shove his way through. Arms grabbed him. A big hand covered his mouth and nose. He could not breathe. He fought and fought until he went limp. Laughing, they tossed him to the ground like a rag doll.

"… *Alex … Alex … ?*"

His eyes flickered open. A hazy face swam into view. "Quick," he gasped, "run!"

"Why?"

Alex glanced around. He saw fruit-laden trees and birds. No Agouti guards.

"Oh!" He sat up, rubbing his sore temple. "How did I get on the ground?"

Yaso squatted beside him. "You fell out the hammock on your head. Serve you right!"

He gripped her arm agitatedly. "Something bad is going to happen to me, Yaso."

"What you expect after you so mean?"

Alex withdrew sullenly. "Well if you're going to be mean back to me, go away."

"Say sorry, and I'll stay."

Alex grimaced. "Sorry I was nasty. It's just that I'm— I'm scared."

"Of what?"

"Of what will happen if I die."

"Stop being so gramatic, Alex, you not gonna die!"

"I'm not being dramatic, Yaso. It could happen." He eyed her warily. "Do you— do you believe dreams can tell the future?"

"Of course! My dreams do tell. And my feelings too." She glared at him.

"Oh." Alex looked at her as if seeing her for the first time. "You mean— Yaso, do you— do you have other powers?"

Yaso hesitated. "Well … I can smell things far, far away, but nobody believe me."

"I can hear things far, far away."

Alex and Yaso stared at each other for a moment, then broke into broad smiles.

"There are others like us, you know," said Alex. "One day, I'm going to search for them."

"Tell me when. I want to come too." Yaso flopped into the hammock. "What's that 'S' with a spiky ball in the centre?" She pointed to a drawing in the dirt.

"The sign of Señora Lagrima's killer! Who put it there?"

"Maybe you. Did you dream about her?"

"No." Alex told her the dream. "It was so real," he said at the end.

"You lucky to see your Papi," said Yaso wistfully. "I never see my family. Maybe 'cause they all burn up."

"I don't think so. I think you have to wish for it at the right time."

A movement caught her eye and Yaso glanced in the direction of the house. "Hey, what Madou flying? A new toy plane?"

Alex turned. Madou was running and holding something high in the air. *Plink, plonk,* he heard very faintly.

"My panman!" Alex sprang up. "COME BACK HERE, MADOU!"

"NO!"

Madou sprinted towards the front of the house, with Alex and Yaso after him. He dashed past the flamboyant tree and straight out the open front gate. "Yaaahhhh, you can't ketch me!" he crowed gleefully over his shoulder, sticking out his tongue at Alex.

"*¡OJO!*" Alex shouted.

"STOP, TEN DOLLA!" Yaso shrieked.

The cartman tried to swerve, but he was too late. Madou crashed headlong into the cart and was pitched to the roadside like a rag doll.

"WHOA, NING-NING!" Ten Dolla hopped off the cart and rushed back towards the crumpled figure. *"YOU TRYING TO MASH UP ME CART? EH? EH?"*

"Shut up, Ten Dolla! You gon scare him!" Yaso screamed.

Alex jiggled Madou's leg. "Dou-Dou! Wake up!" His eyes flickered open and he struggled gamely to rise, only to slump back down.

"Nothing wrong with 'im," said Ten Dolla, "is play 'e playing."

"Look, blood!" Horrified, Yaso pointed to a monstrous gash under Madou's forearm.

"IS NOT MY FAULT! I NOT TAKING BLAME AN' JAIL AGAIN FOR NOBODY!" Ten Dolla bellowed. The scar down the side of his sallow face bulged with fear.

"Yaso, tell Sita to call the doctor. Quick!"

Yaso took off like a shot.

Alex tried once more to rouse Madou. He didn't notice Ten Dolla slinking back to his cart. All he heard was, "Giddyap, Ning-Ning!" Startled, he looked up. The cartman sped away without a backward glance.

Much later, Alex sat on the front step, waiting restlessly. It was after nine-thirty and Yaso was already in bed. The night sky seemed to be acquiring a peculiar purplish hue, as if a storm was brewing. At length, a car pulled into the driveway.

Sita got out. "Thanks again, Dr. Mashado."

The doctor waved.

Quickly, Alex ran to her side. "How is Madou?"

"He in a coma, an' the doctor say if he don't come out soon …"

Alex's heart skipped a beat. "Coma? What do you mean?"

"He not waking up at all, chile, no matter what they do. Oh Lord, what I gon tell his mammy? And what I gon tell Missa Fran? He bound to fire me now." Sita sat down heavily on the front step and covered her face with her hands.

Alex put his arm around her. "Don't cry, Sita. I'll find a way to make everything right again."

"Ah, boy, that sound good, but talk is easy." Sita wiped her eyes. "You find the panman yet?"

"Uh-uh, but I will," said Alex grimly. He knew what he had to do.

NIRVANA

ALEX SPRINTED AWAY AS FAST AS HE COULD. His backpack bounced around uncomfortably, but he gritted his teeth and kept going. All the streetlights were out except for one several blocks away. He slipped and stumbled along the uneven clay brick road until the shadows swallowed up 281 Oleander Drive, then he slowed to a brisk walk.

Apart from the hum of an approaching vehicle and the occasional bark of a neighbourhood dog, his breathing and the faint slap of his runners were the only noises that broke the stillness of the night – until the softest of sounds caught his ears. Alex stopped. The sound stopped. Behind him, it was pitch black. The moon had slipped behind some clouds. He started off. There it was again. Switching on his torchlight, he swung around sharply. In the weak light, he saw the ghostly face of a cougar. It was close enough for him to see the pink nose and white whiskers against its cinnamon fur.

Alex flicked the light on and off. "*¡Arre!* Shoo!"

With a hiss, the cat bared its long canine teeth. "Oh-Oh!"

Alex turned and ran in earnest, fear giving him speed. In the middle of the next block, the cougar pounced on him, knocking him to the ground. Winded, Alex cringed, waiting for its claws to tear his flesh. Instead, it swatted him lightly and bounded off.

A moment later, a familiar blue SUV turned out of the side street Alex had just crossed and headed towards the Changs' house. Dazed, Alex stared at it. "The cougar saved me from the Agoutis!" he murmured.

Blocks away, the SUV stopped. Alex bit his nails worriedly as its taillights went out. "The house is locked. They'll never get in. But what if they do?" He glanced skyward. Purple clouds swirled restlessly. The moon reappeared, bathing Oleander Drive in its light. "I can't turn back now," he muttered. Scrambling up, he hurried towards Banana Circle. Towa-Towa Forest was not far away now.

As he was passing behind Yaso's school, a streak of violet lightning arced down and struck the ground beside him.

"*¡Aiiii!*" Alex yelped, as a shockwave ran through his body.

Instantly, he began to hear whispers. They seemed to come from all around him. Panicking, he raced for the Forest. He got as far as the centre, when a loud thrashing chased his courage completely away. WHOMP! WHOMP! WHOMP! Something huge was thundering towards him. Hoppers, slitherers and crawlers alike stampeded for cover.

Alex threw himself between two buttresses of a silk cotton tree. "Father Kumaka, guardian of life, protect me," he whispered fervently.

The branches of the trees nearby began to quiver. Leaves and twigs flew into the air as if caught in a cyclone. In the trickle of moonlight, Alex spied, emerging from the shadows, a harpy eagle. He froze in horror. The bird's wingspan was wider than the base of the massive silk cotton tree, and its talons looked large enough to hold Alex in their grip. The harpy swooped towards him at incredible speed, its gold-flecked eyes hungry for a kill.

"Quick, curl up!" a voice hissed.

Shaken out of his stupor, Alex curled into a tight ball. His ragged breath was fiery against his skin. A moment later, he felt a rush of wind as something whizzed through the air and rammed into the breast of the bird. With a bloodcurdling shriek, the eagle rose swiftly and was gone.

An eerie silence followed. Alex's heart thumped so wildly, it rocked his entire body. He peered around cautiously. The ground was littered with debris. A leaf drifted down from a swaying overhead branch. Alex slumped against the root of the silk cotton tree. "Thank you," he breathed. Grabbing his torchlight, he stepped back on the trail and brushed the leaves and dirt from his clothes.

"Going my way?" a deep honeyed voice called out.

Alex started. He waved the torch in the direction of the voice. Shadows danced between the trees. He caught a glimpse of a pair of eyes gleaming like tiny moons in the bushes, and crouched, ready to defend himself.

"Come out of there whoever you are," he ordered,

"or else I'll— I'll—" He tried to sound as fierce as possible.

"Okay, partner, you got me." The voice chuckled, and out came a silvery grey animal.

"The magic fox!" Alex gasped.

"Check the tail, dude. Does it hang like a fox's? I think not! I'm a canine mutt and proud to be one."

On closer examination, Alex could see patches of white, black and faun all over its silvery grey coat. Its eyes did not slant upwards, its muzzle was not as pointed and its fuzzy tail turned gently upwards at the tip. What's more, it was much bigger than any fox Alex had ever seen. "You *are* a mutt."

"Yup."

"Is this a trick?" Alex edged back towards the silk cotton tree. He shone the torchlight beyond the dog. "Who's talking?"

"Me."

"B-b-but dogs can't talk."

"Dogs can't talk? Yak, yak, yak! Don't crack me up!" the dog squealed, rolling on the ground with laughter. "Which dimension are you from, dude?"

Alex rubbed his eyes vigorously. "I must be asleep."

"Pinch me, if you think you're dreaming," the dog offered, a mischievous look in his hazel eyes, "or, seeing as how I'm part Doberman Pinscher, why don't *I* pinch *you* instead? Yak, yak, yak, yak! Pinscher, pinch, get it?"

"No, no!" Alex backed away hastily. "But you can't be normal. I never heard a dog say anything but 'wroff!' and 'Grrrrr!'"

"And most humans never say anything to me but 'nice doggie' and 'fetch!'" the dog responded jovially, sitting back on its haunches, "which means *you* ain't normal."

"Oh." Alex blinked, surprised. A memory came flooding back. "It was the purple lightning! That's when I first started hearing animal voices!"

"More power to ya, dude, pun intended, yak, yak, yak! I'm with the United Earth Federation, Canine Division. The name's Nirvana, but you can call me Nirv. What's yours?"

"Alex Springfeather. I'm Waspachu of the Cougar Clan. Most people think we're Arawak because they think all Waspachus are dead, but that's not true."

"Tell it like it is, preacher-man."

Alex grinned. "You're *Norteamericano*. You're not from here."

"Sure I am. I'm from here, there and e-ve-ry-where, but if you wanna know where I last went, just check, just check my ac-cent," Nirvana rapped, bobbing his head in time.

Alex cracked up. "You're *muy loco!*"

"Glad ya like me. So where are you off to?"

"Dury Lane."

"Follow me." Nirvana inclined his head towards the thicket. "I know a short cut."

Alex suddenly grew cautious again. "I— I prefer to use the trail."

"Still don't trust me, eh? Even after I saved your life. Well, see ya later, alligator."

The dog disappeared into the thicket.

"Wait!"

Nirvana poked his head back out of the shrubs, grinning. "Changed your mind, eh? Hang on to my tail, then, and let's go!"

They started off at a moderate trot. "Did the silk cotton tree send you?" asked Alex eagerly. "Are you my Spirit Animal?"

"Keep both eyes shut, Alex Springfeather. You don't wanna get hurt by flying branches."

Faster and faster they went until their feet barely touched the ground. Alex could not resist peeping. His eyes streamed. Everything was a blur, so he could not be sure, but it seemed the trees and shrubs were moving their branches aside to let them pass.

Without warning, Nirvana stopped. Alex went sailing over his head and landed with a thud on his backpack. He struggled to sit up, more shaken than hurt.

"Whatappen?" he asked thickly.

Before the dog could explain himself, a large hyacinth macaw with brilliant blue feathers swooped down and dropped something, stirring up a lot of dust.

"OUCH!" yelped the thing.

"Yaso?" Alex scrabbled over to her on hands and knees.

She looked shell-shocked. "A m-macaw just p-pick me up from the ground and f-fly me here fast, fast!"

"Found her tumbling through the woods, Nirv," the macaw explained, circling overhead.

"It's okay, Cocoa, I'll take care of her," said Nirvana reassuringly.

"What are you doing out of the house?" asked Alex, alarmed. "Are the Agoutis after you?"

"H-how can a bird fly me?" Yaso spread her arms helplessly.

Alex glanced over his shoulder. The macaw was making a beeline for a pile of logs. "She must be a spirit animal like Nirv," he answered impatiently. "So, what happened?"

Yaso stared at him blankly. "A spirit?"

Nirvana stepped from behind Alex. "You okay? No damage, I hope. Cocoa is the best in our Avian Division, but her style is crude."

Yaso's eyes fell on him, and her mouth opened and closed like a fish. "The magic fox from my dream!" she gasped.

"He's not a magic fox, Yaso, he's a dog, and his name is Nirvana."

Suddenly Nirvana exclaimed, "Your elbow, it's bleeding!"

"Huh?" Alex twisted his arm and saw a nasty gash.

"Sorry, dude, my fault." Nirvana licked the spot.

"It disappeared!" Alex ran his hand over his arm. "No mark, nothing!"

"Didn't mean to stop so suddenly." Nirvana looked across the clearing. "It was the charm of the place that got me, man. Happens every time."

Alex followed his gaze and what he saw left him spellbound. Partially hidden by trees, not far in the distance, was a lake of the most peculiar shades of magenta and turquoise. A mysterious island wrapped in wisps of mist sat in its centre. A strange golden glow lit up the dusky sky.

"¡*Vaya!* What is that?" he gasped, springing up.

"Who put a magic land there?" breathed Yaso, catching sight of it.

"That's my home, Swan Island," said Nirvana proudly. "Come and meet my folks. It won't take a minute. Dury Lane is just a spit away from here."

Alex eyed the island uneasily. "Yaso and I went everywhere in the forest and we never saw a place like that before. We must be someplace else."

"Turn towards your left, dude, and take a good look."

"The trail!" Alex exclaimed, spotting the familiar path through the trees. "But—"

Yaso, who had been looking from one to the other, perplexed, finally asked, "Alex, you and the magic fox talking?"

"Can't you hear him?"

Yaso shook her head, crestfallen. "I din't know you can talk to animals."

"On Swan Island, you'll both have the power to do anything you want," Nirvana butted in temptingly. "Everything is possible."

"What he saying?" asked Yaso impatiently.

"He said we'll have the power to do anything we want on the island, but we can't go."

"Why not?"

Alex cast a wary glance at Nirvana. "We have things to do," he said tightly.

"If you don't want to go, I'll go alone," Yaso decided, gazing at the island longingly.

"You can't."

"I'll leave you two to work things out," said Nirvana, grinning. He trotted over to the macaw.

The moment he was out of earshot, Alex hissed, "Did you forget you're supposed to cover for me, in case Sita wakes up?"

"You said you coming back by morning. If Sita can sleep while the people searching the house, nothing going to wake her up before sun up."

"They got in?"

"Uh-huh. Through the kitchen window. I smelled trouble and woke up, and when they searching your room, I listened at the door. The man say, 'Flown out the coop,' or something like that, and the lady say, 'What a crafty one, but we know where he going. We can still get him before they do.' Then they jump in the car and drived off."

Alex felt a stab of fear.

"Who's 'they', Alex? Who else looking for you?"

"I don't know, and I don't know how the Agoutis know I'm going to find Ten Dolla." He thought for a moment. "Can you use your smell power to tell if I'm in trouble?"

"I s'pose. Yeh, I can."

"Okay. Go back home, and if you sense anything, get help. I'll— Wait! I have an idea!" Alex delved into his backpack and pulled out a plastic bag filled with the yellow fluffy flesh of a fruit. He opened the bag and stuck it in Yaso's face.

She wrinkled her nose. "Eeuuuh! Stinking Toe."

"This is three pods. I broke them open at home. I was planning to eat on the way, but as soon as I get onto Ten Dolla's cart, I'll start dropping bits of it. This way you can smell your way to me quicker, if they catch me."

"Don't go, Alex, *please*. I smell death!"

"It's the Stinking Toe," Alex joked, but there was a tremor in his voice. "I have to go, Yaso, you know that. I have to believe I can do it, and you must believe too."

"Okay, okay."

Alex checked his watch. 12:05 a.m. "Time to go. The rum shop is closed."

"But s'pose—"

"Shhh!" Alex put a finger to his lips and pointed over his shoulder.

"… only one with six powers. I am sure," Cocoa was saying softly to Nirvana.

"What they saying?" whispered Yaso eagerly.

"… our Link," Nirvana murmured in reply. "We shall see."

Alex glanced over his shoulder to find them studying him. Nirvana approached. "Ready to go?" he asked cheerfully.

There was a soft rustle of wings and Cocoa soared skywards. "Byeee! Enjoy the island!"

"We can't go," said Alex firmly. "I'm meeting someone on Dury Lane, and Yaso has to go home."

"If you mean Ten Dolla and his faithful donkey, Ning-Ning, ya got lots of time, dude. He's not even on the road yet."

Alex gaped at him in shock. "You know about him too? But how?"

"Know about who? Know about who?" Yaso badgered, trying desperately to follow the conversation.

"I know a lot of things, Alex Springfeather, and so do you. Use the power of i-sight. Let your inner eye follow him and see for yourself."

"But I— you— It doesn't work anymore," Alex ended lamely.

"Only fear stops it. Are you a scaredy cat?"

Alex glared at the dog. Covering his eyes lightly with his fingers, he checked. After a while, he dropped his hands. "I saw the police taking him to the station for fighting in the rum shop. That was a while ago."

"That's right," Nirvana confirmed. "He won't be here for another half hour at least."

Alex checked the time. And checked again. "My new watch has stopped working," he groaned. "It's stuck at 12:05."

"Mine too!" said Yaso, frowning.

"You're in a zero zone now. Time stops around here. You can stay on the island forever and still get where you want to go on time. So, let's bounce, man!"

Alex hesitated. "That's strange."

Yaso tugged at his sleeve. "What's strange?"

"He said we can stay on the island for as long as we want, because time stops here."

Yaso's face lit up like a thousand candle lights. "You mean I can go and have fun, and still reach home at the same time as if I go now?"

"It happened in Cree Kee Forest too," Alex muttered. "Nirv, how did you stop it?"

"I didn't. These zones have been here, and in other parts of the world, since ... well since time began."

"So, why doesn't everybody know about it?"

"The island! It's gone," Yaso suddenly howled. "You talked too much, Alex."

Alex swivelled round. The lake had indeed vanished, and in its place was a shadowy glen. "What's going on?" he whispered. "Are you doing magic, Nirv?"

"Those whose minds are clouded see only a swamp and avoid it. Clear your minds and you will see again. C'mon, close your eyes and count to ten. Put aside those worrisome thoughts. Focus on the island and the fun you'll have."

Suddenly, Alex really wanted to go. He explained quickly to Yaso, and together, they shut their eyes.

"It's back!" Alex whooped, opening his eyes on the count of ten.

"Yeh," Yaso breathed, "with a— with a—"

This time there was a floating pavilion, with an arched bridge connecting the island to the mainland.

"Is it real?" asked Alex.

"Find out for yourself." Nirvana trotted ahead.

"Race you there!" Alex yelled.

As they drew closer, they heard laughter. "Is it a big playground?" asked Yaso breathlessly.

"If that's what you want it to be." Suddenly Nirvana bellowed, "YOU GO, GIRL!"

A sleek black and white dolphin rose out of the water to a mighty height, flipped over with effortless grace and dove back into the depths.

"That's Viva," he said in a voice filled with admiration.

Alex and Yaso charged up the arched bridge to catch a better glimpse of her.

"*Qui va la*? Who goes there, child or grown-up?" a fatherly voice asked with mock severity.

Neither Alex nor Yaso heard. Viva came up again and somersaulted through the air.

The voice repeated emphatically, and then thundered, "I SAID, WHO GOES THERE, CHILD OR GROWN-UP?"

"Oh-oh." Nirvana retreated hastily.

A wave of water swept over Alex and Yaso, drenching them.

"Hey!" They swung round angrily and came face to face with the owner of the voice.

"A talkin' monster goose!" Yaso cried, stumbling backwards and tripping over Alex's feet.

"Alex, Yaso, this is Solo, Keeper of the Gate," announced Nirvana dramatically, "and he's not a goose, but a Black-necked Swan. The most elegant you will ever see in South America."

Solo bowed graciously. "For the last time, who goes there?"

Only then did Alex and Yaso notice the gap between the bridge and the pavilion.

"That's right, dudes. No one gets into the pavilion until Solo says so. He takes his role as Keeper very seriously. Just say 'child'. It's like a password."

"Child!" they chorused.

In an instant, the bird was transformed. He stretched his sleek ebony neck majestically upwards, and swept his massive snow white wings outwards full span, scattering colourful droplets of water everywhere. "WELCOME TO SWAN ISLAND. MAY THIS JEWEL OF THE FOREST BE YOUR HOME AWAY FROM HOME!" he boomed.

Flapping his wings powerfully, he propelled the bridge forward. It clicked into place, but a mahogany door, with no visible knob or handle, prevented them from going further. Its surface shimmered with every breath they took.

"Go on, touch it," urged Nirvana.

Alex stuck a finger out and poked it, barely. A tiny hole formed. Ripples fanned outwards, gathering speed as the hole expanded, until the entire door vanished with a pop. A stream of golden light blinded them.

"YOU MAY NOW ENTER THE PAVILION OF RECORDS."

Alex took a bold step in and landed on something soft. It bore him swiftly forward. Shielding his eyes, he looked down to see what it was. His heart lurched. There was nothing beneath his feet! He was deposited gently in the centre of the room and a moment later, a swishing sound heralded the arrival of Yaso.

"The room don't have no floor," she said nervously.

"I know!"

"Just relax and enjoy the ride," Nirvana advised, as he swept past them.

Chimes tinkled. All at once the light was sucked out of the room, rolling like a wave to a pinpoint.

"*Aleeeeee*— !" Yaso's voice trailed away, like a person falling off a cliff.

"Yaso?" Alex felt around for her in the darkness. "NIRV!" The Doberman pressed his cold, reassuring nose against Alex's hand. "Where's Yaso?"

"We left her behind to do her own thing."

"*Behind?*"

"Look up, dude, don't miss the fireworks!"

Alex looked up. Lights like fireflies danced towards them, growing larger by the second. "Stars! I'm in space!" He looked down. "Hey! There's nothing holding me up!"

"Relax, bro, just go with the flow."

"*Bienvenidos*, Alex Springfeather, welcome! We've been waiting for you." The soft bubbly voice seemed to come from everywhere at once.

Alex's fear dissolved in a rush of pleasure. "*Gracias, señora!*" he gushed. To Nirvana, he whispered, "What does she mean? Who's been waiting? How does she know my name?"

111

The Doberman's eyes twinkled. "Take a guess."

"She's an angel! Does she have wings and everything?"

"Wings," the voice replied merrily, "are best left to those who desire to move quickly. They don't suit me at all."

Alex squinted upwards. "Where are you? I can't see you."

"You shall, later, if you be patient. We will now introduce you to the work of the United Earth Federation, which runs Swan Island, and perhaps you will consider joining us?"

In a flash of lightning, several doors sliced through the space encircling Alex and Nirvana. They pulsated temptingly.

"You have seven options, Alex Springfeather, seven different lands from which you may choose one," the voice explained.

"Lands?" He spun around and around looking from portal to portal.

"Yes, lands."

Alex walked to the nearest one. He reached out, expecting it to swirl open like the one at the pavilion's entrance. Instead, his arm was yanked in right up to his elbow. "*¡Aiii!*" he exclaimed, snatching it back.

"You must choose now," the voice said.

"Go on," Nirvana urged, "it'll be fun. I'll be with you. Pick a number."

"Ah— four?" said Alex tentatively.

"FOUR!" Nirvana echoed loudly.

"Your choice is four," the female voice confirmed.

The sound of rushing wind filled his ears, and a moment later, Alex was sucked into a vessel that was familiar, yet different from anything he could imagine. He was tossed into what felt like an old washing machine, jiggled about like a rag, until at last he was spewed out.

Reeling from shock, Alex found himself bumbling about in some kind of alleyway, surrounded by tall brick buildings. The sound of traffic and sirens droned in the distance. A stone ricocheted off a nearby wall and hit him.

"Hey!" he cried out. "Owoooo!" he heard, deafeningly close to his ears.

A harsh voice rang through the air. "What was that?"

"Only a mad dog howling for the dead," another answered.

"Somebody shut that mutt up!"

"A word of advice, Alex. Vocals are for barking only," Nirvana said. He zipped behind an old crate a split second before a stone hit it with a loud *pak!* "Just project your thoughts and I'll hear ya."

Nirvana's familiar silvery coat was so close, Alex could see tiny individual hairs on his legs. "I'm ... I'm in your body!" he gasped.

"Yup! Beats virtual reality any day."

"DEATH TO THE ENEMIES OF OUR BROTHER!" a high pitched voice suddenly screamed.

Two gangs of teens charged towards each other, one side wearing red bandanas, the other wearing blue.

Their faces were contorted with hatred. Knives and broken bottles glinted in the afternoon light.

"Do something, Nirv, quick! Bite somebody, call the police! They're going to kill each other!"

Calmly, Nirvana stepped out into the open again, and said, "Silver light, deflect their might!"

His entire body glowed like a light bulb for a split second, then a blast of silvery light shot out. It splintered into several long, mirror-like pieces and fell between the gangs just as they lunged at each other. Their knives, broken bottles, bats, crashed into mirror images of themselves. Instantly, the pieces of light dissolved.

Alex and Nirvana watched as gang members on both sides dropped to their knees, clutching their bodies in pain.

"What happened?" asked one hoarsely.

"Silver ghosts! I saw them!"

"Me too," croaked another, staring blankly at a spot in front of him.

"They turned our weapons against us!"

"I feel pain everywhere, but there's no blood!" the youngest gang member muttered. He was no more than thirteen. "I told you revenge was going to land us in worse trouble," he spat at his leader. "This is a sign! I'm leaving!"

"Me too!" came a chorus of voices.

"Wait, you cowards!"

"Not me!"

"Uh-uh!"

"What for?"

In no time, the gang members fled the scene. Alex shook with mirth and Nirvana's body quivered.

"Don't think they'll be fighting again anytime soon!"

"Don't think so. Was that fun, or what?"

"It was great! I felt like I was doing it too."

"You were, dude. This power is now yours."

"You're like a guardian angel, Nirv!"

"Just doing my job," said Nirvana modestly. "Ready to go?"

"If you are."

Nirvana returned to the exact spot where they first appeared and stroked the air with his paw. There was a rumbling sound and the shimmering portal became visible. Nirvana hopped through and the rushing wind swept them up. Suddenly, there was a ear-splitting *POP!*

"Thank you for journeying with us, Alex Springfeather."

Then there was a gentle, drifting silence.

When Alex opened his eyes, he was slumped in the centre of the golden room of the Pavilion of Records. The room looked quite ordinary now. Nirvana was spread out flat on the wooden floor, slobbering all over his face.

"Okay now?" he asked.

"Okay," said Alex weakly.

He straightened up. Out of nowhere, a rosy mist formed in front of him. It grew and stretched and stretched and grew until at last a shape appeared. He saw big kindly eyes and a loving smile first, then the curly ridges on its shell. An elephant-sized pink snail filled the room.

"My name is Maya," said a familiar voice softly. "I was your pavilion guide."

"Oh! I thought you were a lady," Alex burst out without thinking.

"Ah, but she is," Nirvana cut in, "the most gracious you will ever find. Maya is our memory. She's so old and wise even Mother Earth bows in respect to her."

"So, how old are you?" asked Alex brazenly. He got up to inspect the creature.

"Older than the mountains."

Alex's eyes widened. "Then you must be a million years old!"

"Oh, much, much older than that," Maya confessed, "but I slept through the Ice Age, so I feel much younger."

Alex gawked. "You mean you were in a coma and didn't wake up for millions of years?"

"Something like that."

"I have a friend in a coma," Alex blurted out.

"I'm sorry to hear that! What happened?"

Alex felt the sadness descend. "Do we have to talk about it now?"

"Not at all!" said Maya agreeably. "Actually, I'd rather talk about you. The UEF would like to help you with your quest. We almost lost you back there on Oleander Drive, but Paima from our Feline Division, saved the day. We wouldn't want something like that to happen again."

Alex gaped. "You've been tracking me! But why? I'm not important."

"To us you are." Nirvana rose and shook himself. "Wanna see the island now and meet others like yourself?"

"Yes!" Alex went to collect his backpack.

"He's the best chance we've got, isn't he?" Maya whispered to Nirvana.

"Possibly our last chance," Nirvana whispered back.

SWAN ISLAND

MINUTES LATER, NIRVANA BOUNDED OUT OF THE PAVILION of Records with Alex in tow. Maya followed at a snail's pace. Hopping off the bridge, Alex ran forward a few paces and stopped, surprised. Kneeling down, he scooped up a handful of sand. It glittered temptingly. Gingerly, he stuck out his tongue and tasted it.

"It's sugar!" he exclaimed.

"Golden crystal. Nothing but the best for us, dude." The Doberman flopped onto the sand to enjoy Alex's pleasure.

Alex's eyes gleamed. "We could fill bags and bags of it and sell it in the market. We'd be rich."

"Not with *this* sugar. Mix it with anything but love, and it'll go sour."

Alex dropped the sugar sand and looked around eagerly. There were all kinds of trees – palms, flamboyants, golden showers and many more – and they all had one thing in common. They glowed as if lit from the inside, turning night into day on the island.

"Oh, look!" he shouted.

Viva was pushing a squirrel on a log diagonally across the sparkling channel which split the upper part of the island in two.

Nirvana turned his head. "That's lazy Lola – always looking for a quick way to get around."

Alex laughed out loud when the log rolled in the middle of the channel, tipping Lola into the water.

"More haste, less speed y'know, Little Lo!" Nirvana called out.

The shamefaced squirrel scrambled back onto the log. In the distance, not far from her destination, an elephant and a mongoose conversed amiably.

"What's an elephant doing here?"

"Oh, we have visitors from all over the world."

There were all kinds of animals. Alex spotted a tapir, an ocelot, a raccoon. In the water, manatees and otters frolicked with flying fish.

"This should be called Animal Island, not Swan Island," Alex joked.

Nirvana grinned. "Good point, but the island wasn't created for the animals. They are here as teachers and guides. It was created especially for dudes like you. See, wisdom and power are greatest wherever time stops, so it's a perfect place for children of the prophesy to—" His words were drowned out by a flock of giant Black-necked Swans swooping past with squealing riders on their backs.

They circled back. Nirvana stood up and wagged his tail vigorously at them. "That's our sky tour!" he shouted above the noise.

"I want to try that!" A distant burst of laughter caught Alex's ear and he swung in the direction of the sound. "Yaso! What's she doing?"

Nirvana followed his gaze. "Playing psyk. Wanna try your luck?"

Alex's eyes lit up. "Okay."

Across a rainbow bridge, Yaso and a group of boys and girls were rushing around with their eyes glued to a couple of glittering crystal balls twirling in mid-air above their heads. One of the balls carried flashing spikes. It shot a ray out and hit Yaso, and up popped a misty image of a yak. Yaso ran headlong into it, bounced off and went crashing to the ground.

Alex dashed towards her hooting with laughter. "Yaaah, that's so *funny*!"

"Think you can do better?" asked Nirvana, catching up with him on the bridge.

"Of course. I'm quicker. Those rays will never catch me."

"Famous last words! Reema!" Nirvana approached a girl in a wheelchair. "My bud here wants to show what he can do."

"Okay," she said readily, preparing to roll herself out of the circle.

"No, don't take her out," whispered Alex craftily, "take out one of the others."

"Take out one of the others, he says! Yak, yak, yak!" Nirvana cackled. "He thinks that will improve his odds! Man, you couldn't beat her even if you tried all night. She's the ruling one-on-one champion! You're looking at our psyk instructor, dude. Introduce yourself around."

His face hot with embarrassment, Alex greeted the group.

"Where did you disappear to?" asked Yaso breathlessly, shaking golden sand out of her clothing.

"You're a first timer," drawled Reema.

Alex nodded.

"It's easy," Yaso boasted.

"Easy to fall on your bumsy!"

"You gon fall too," Yaso retorted, making a face at him.

"Not me!"

"Button up, ya wallas," said Reema amiably but firmly. Alex shot her a startled look. She looked frail, yet she radiated an inner power. "Alex," she continued, "see that circle with the three sets of lines on either side? That's our field. You must draw the balls from the centre of the circle into your zone to win, in other words, over the first line."

"And what about the other lines?"

"Forget about them for the moment. Zones two and three are for advanced players."

"Okay, but how do I move the balls?"

"Focus on the octron – that's the crystal ball without spikes. Draw it to yourself using your will. That's what we call psyking. The xytron will follow – that's the smaller ball with spikes. But first you have to get past those spikes. If you look at them or think about them, they'll send out rays to zap you, and if you get hit, whatever is in your mind will appear and smack you one. Then it'll be the other person's turn. Three smacks and you're out. That's one-a-side, but you'll be playing two-a-side for starters. It's easier.

One person to draw the xytron away, the other to psyk the octron. Which would you like— "

"One-a-side," said Alex promptly.

"Ha, ha, ha!" Yaso cackled.

"Ha, ha yourself," Alex shot back.

"I was giving you a choice between taming the xytron or psyking the octron in two-a-side," said Reema, amused. "A beginner playing one-a-side would have to be a Speedy Gonzalez to survive, or they'll get whacked silly."

"Maybe I don't have to be a Speedy Gonzalez, and maybe I won't be whacked silly."

By now, everyone was sniggering. Alex grinned back at them brashly.

"Okay, it's your funeral." Reema and Nirvana's eyes met and something passed between them. "Let's go."

"Who am I playing?"

"Me, of course." Reema wheeled herself back into the circle.

"*You*?" Alex sobered up at once. "That's not fair, you're the instructor."

"Pawk, pawk," Yaso teased.

With a smouldering glance at her, Alex said, "Okay, I'll do it."

"Fine, best three out of five. Alex, as the challenger, you go first."

"Let the games begin!" Nirvana proclaimed dramatically.

Alex went to stand in the circle. Taking a deep breath, he looked up. Straight away, a bolt of red light shot from one of the xytron's spikes and zapped him in the chest. It felt no stronger than the light from a torch, yet almost right away, a vision of his mother appeared inches from his nose. It smacked him and disappeared.

Alex lay on the ground staring at the spot, unable to believe how real the hologram seemed. He felt a yearning so strong, he whacked the ground angrily, and sprang up.

"NOT FAIR! I WASN'T READY!"

"If you focus on the xytron, you'll get zapped," Reema repeated. "Look past the xytron, straight at the octron. Like so."

She rolled into the centre of the circle and stared up at the crystal balls with a distant look. Within seconds, the octron moved. Slowly she backed up her wheelchair, never altering her gaze. As the xytron whirled madly around the octron, it spat and zapped once in a while, but always missed her. She made it look easy. After she rolled into her zone, she took her gaze off them to acknowledge the cheers from the small crowd that had gathered, and the crystal balls moved swiftly back to the centre of the circle.

"Watch and weep, dude, the xytron tamer is *smokin'*," yelled Nirvana.

Whose side is he on? Alex wondered crossly. Going again, he tried his best to focus on the octron, but the xytron's flashing spikes kept drawing his eyes. Next thing he knew, he was rushing helter-skelter around the circle, desperately dodging bolts of light shooting out like bullets from a machine gun. He knew he couldn't keep this up for long and was actually glad when a ray finally hit. An image of the silver panman bashed him this time.

Exhausted and gasping for breath, he lay on the golden crystals wishing they would turn into quicksand and swallow him up. He peeked at his audience: Yaso was rolling on the ground with laughter, Nirvana was yak-yakking so hard, he looked like he was about to have a fit and Reema was biting her lips and trying so hard to hide her laughter, her face was contorted into a most horrible grimace, while tears streamed freely down her cheeks. He couldn't bear to look further.

Rising from the sand, he put on a brave face and watched Reema psyk the crystal balls into her zone with ease for a second time, and all too soon, it was his turn again. He took a deep breath.

"Three smacks and you out, remember!" Yaso hissed, setting everybody off laughing again. I should just pretend to twist my ankle so I can get away from here, Alex thought desperately.

"You can do it, just let go of the ego," said Reema encouragingly.

"I don't know what you mean," said Alex sullenly. "I'm sure I can do it, but when I try, it doesn't work. How do you do it?"

"First off, I don't care if I win or lose, so with nothing to bother me, my mind becomes strong," she replied frankly. "Secondly, I think only of what I want, not what might happen."

Alex eyed her with growing respect. Reema was not much older than him, but she sounded a lot smarter. "Can you explain some more?"

"Let's see ..." Reema scratched her chin. "If you're dying of thirst in a desert, mate, will a rhino by the waterhole stop you from drinking?"

Alex blinked a few times then his brow cleared. "I see what you mean!"

He took up his position in the circle once more and fixed his gaze on the centre of the octron as if nothing else mattered. The spikes flashed and winked, but now they held no charm. He began to move slowly backwards towards his zone, willing the octron to follow and, amazingly, it began to move! He was so delighted, he lost focus briefly, and in that instant a multicoloured ray of light shot from one of the xytron's spikes, zapping him on the shoulder. A hologram of the Agouti people popped up. Alex caught his breath, but ignored it. He kept his eyes and mind on the octron, and *poof!* the hologram vanished. Before he knew it, he was crossing into his zone. A cheer went up.

"Well, Reema," Nirvana whispered, "what do you think?"

"Definitely an 'A' in the test of will."

Alex stood there in a fog of happiness while the crowd of onlookers showered praise on him.

"Honourable elder brother," said Yaso, beaming, "I proud of you."

Eventually, everyone went back to their own games, and Nirvana, Alex and Yaso set off to explore the island.

"Not bad," Nirvana remarked to Alex. "You managed all right in the end."

"I did more than manage," Alex boasted.

"Yeh, he did good!" said Yaso, slapping him on the back.

"That's a toddlers' game, though. The real challenge is tree dodging. I had a little bet with Reema. She thinks you can handle the big league, but considering the spot of trouble you had at the beginning psyking, I seriously doubt it. She thinks you can win. I think it's a waste of time your even trying. You're too easily distracted."

Yaso stared at the dog as if she couldn't believe her ears.

"If you think so, then you don't know me," Alex snapped, his pride wounded.

"Wanna prove it?"

"Let's go."

They took an elephant ride to the hills, where groves of luminous trees grew. Large swaths separated them. As he slid off the prickly back of the elephant onto the sand, Alex realized he never asked what the game was about.

"So what's tree dodging? And where are the players?" he asked gruffly.

"Arriving now."

A bearded man came over the crest of the hill in the company of four youths. Two of them suddenly broke away and charged down the slope.

"Is it a race?" asked Alex.

Before Nirvana could answer, a huge teddy bear of a man popped up beside them. "Alex Springfeather, the man himself! Splendificent!" he gushed. "It is an honour to have a descendant of the Invisible People in our midst. And my dear Yaso! A pleasure to have a daughter of the Himalayas. The powers that lie within those mountains must lie within you! Welcome!"

As he spoke, tiny leaves sprouted from his bushy eyebrows, while his complexion, at first dark and lined, was slowly becoming smooth and spotted like the bark of a frangipani tree. They stared at the apparition, transfixed – not because he had travelled half the length of a football field in the time it took to inhale, or because of the way he babbled through his flowery beard, or even because he looked like a walking tree. Their eyes were glued to his faded brown overalls, which bulged and twisted as if something fierce was struggling to get out.

"Goat got your tongues?"

Alex blinked rapidly. "Wh— who are you?"

"Morph Al, tree dodging instructor, at your service." A twig shot from his hand and scratched Alex's arm as he bowed.

"*¡Aiii!*" Alex backed away.

"He's a alien!" shouted Yaso gleefully.

"Young lady, I'll have you know I'm a bona fide arbomorph, not an extraterrestrial."

Roots snaked indignantly out of Morph Al's sandaled toes, at which point, Alex and Yaso fell into helpless laughter, a condition which worsened when

Morph Al got infected and joined in with a riotous cackle.

A boy in breeches and a brilliant red sash ran up. "I am Andreas and he is Genjo," he said breathlessly, pointing to a boy lying flat on the sand panting.

The rest of the group had arrived. A slight girl in a sarong and a hibiscus in her hair skipped up to Alex and Yaso. "Hi," she said brightly, "I name Kapua."

"And this is Canila, our reigning champion," said Nirvana, grinning affectionately at a slender girl with dreadlocks wrapped in an orange headscarf. "Everyone, meet Alex and Yaso, the newest additions to our family."

"Right!" Morph Al rubbed his hands together. "Teams, are you ready?"

"Hey," said Alex, startled, "we don't know anything about the game. We just got here."

"Yes, yes, but I'd heard—" he hesitated, eyeing Nirvana. The dog shook his head ever so slightly. "I see. In that case, I hope you at least know that in this particular obstacle race, the only way a runner stays in one piece is by sensing which way the trees will move."

"The trees *move*?" Alex and Yaso chorused.

Morph Al cocked a leafy eyebrow. "But of course! They're all mutant varieties of the common Amazonian crawling tree. I redesigned their genetic codes myself."

"So— so they move onto the tracks there, you mean?" Alex pointed to the broad swaths between the trees.

"The track, dear boy, runs through the trees. The swath between the trees is reserved for the repair squads. Now— "

"Repair squads? To repair what?" Yaso looked dazed.

"The usual: fractures, bumps, scratches, that sort of thing."

"*Fractures?*" By now, Alex and Yaso were gaping at their instructor in horror.

"Alex, let's not play this game," Yaso whispered.

Alex glanced over at Nirvana. The dog covered his eyes with his paws. "I'm not backing out. I'm going to win," he whispered back defiantly.

"Well, I not going home looking like a hospittle case," said Yaso out loud.

"Not to worry," said Morph Al humorously, "to dispel all fears, we give crash courses in repairs, from broken thumbs to shredded bums! Kapua! Genjo! Andreas! Canila! My faithful followers, let's show them, shall we?"

Without further ado, he grabbed his own upper arm and yanked it hard. There was a sharp snap and the arm fell to his side at an awkward angle. Calmly, Morph Al removed a stopwatch from his overalls with his other hand, handed it to Genjo and sat on the ground.

"Did you see that?" Alex gasped. "He— he—"

"Let's go, Canila!" Morph Al ordered.

Canila rushed forward and dropped to her knees beside him.

"Alex, Yaso, watch carefully. If a repair job exceeds twenty seconds, points will be taken off."

He signalled to Canila, who passed a hand over his shoulder and proceeded to hum like a busy bee. A short while later, the shoulder suddenly snapped back into place all by itself.

"Time?" said Morph Al.

"Eleven seconds," said Genjo promptly.

"Right on the button, as usual!"

Canila sat back on her heels, a satisfied smile lighting up her face.

"How did she do that?" Alex breathed in wonder.

"The question, young man, should be, 'How soon will I be able to do that?'" Morph Al said dryly.

"How soon will I be able to do that?" Alex echoed.

"In a minute." He yanked his shoulder out again.

"You just like the Shaolin monks," said Yaso admiringly. "Don't it hurt?"

"Not at all," said Morph Al airily. "Not something a novice should attempt, however. Your turn, Andreas."

Eighteen seconds later, Morph Al's shoulder was back in place.

"How long did it take you to learn?" Alex asked Andreas curiously.

"After fifth time, I do it, but Canila do it first time."

Alex turned to Morph Al eagerly. "Can I try now?"

"Okay, boyo, let's see what you got," and Morph Al yanked his shoulder out for third time.

After a brief hesitation, Alex stuck his hands out straight over the shoulder.

"No, no, not like that, you're not warming your hands over a coal fire, you're working with energy. Harness your power! Use your extrasensory receptors!"

And Morph Al babbled on about different kinds of humming and healing until Alex's head was swimming, but when Morph Al finally said, "Go!" Alex's mind became quite clear. Passing his hands over the arbomorph's shoulder, he began to hum in just the right way. Moments later, the shoulder jerked back up.

"Irie, Alex, irie!" said Canila excitedly.

"Perfectico!" Morph Al exclaimed, wiggling it around. "Time, Genjo?"

There was a moment's silence.

"Nine seconds, sensei."

"Nine?" Morph Al looked over at Nirvana, who was relaxing in a comfortable hollow he'd dug for himself. "He broke Canila's record!" he gasped. The leaves growing out of his brow and scalp withered and dropped off. "You know what this means?"

"I do." Nirvana promptly dashed off behind a passing butterfly the size of a breadfruit leaf.

Morph Al clapped Alex on his back so hard, he had a coughing fit. "Well done," he said, "extremely well done! Yaso, your turn."

Yaso, feeling the pressure of following such a performance, made it just under the 20 second limit her third time around.

"I want to run, anyway," she said with an embarrassed shrug.

"Me too," said Alex.

Andreas eyed them pityingly. "You will be smashed."

"Well then," Morph Al clapped his hands. "Team one: Kapua and Genjo. Team two: Canila and Alex. Team three: Andreas and Yaso. Any objections?"

Everyone shook their heads.

"Fine. Runners, when you hear this … " Morph Al reached down, pulled a long and slender root out of his little toe and cracked it, sending the teams scattering, "off you go."

The sharp noise brought Nirvana scampering back from his game with the butterfly. "All set?"

"Yes, yes. Nirv, you take the finish line. I'll be up on the hill. Runners, remember if you end up with both feet on the swath, disqualified. Repairers, if you enter the woods before your team-mate goes down, disqualified. All clear?"

"Yes!" the six players chorused.

Alex, Yaso and Genjo ran up the slope to the top where the orange flag was posted. Morph Al was already there, all signs of tree growth gone.

"Ready?"

They nodded.

He took them to their respective starting points and said, "Brave young sister and brothers: the rash usually crash, so use intuition and complete the mission." Holding the snaking root aloft, he yelled, "Get set!"

The runners stared straight ahead intently, muscles taut, poised for a quick take off. Alex caught a glimpse of the finish line when a gust of wind ruffled the trees, and wondered if the others had butterflies in their stomach too, thinking about bloody noses and twisted body parts.

There was a loud report and Alex shot into his grove, only to find that the trees didn't crawl at all. They moved with surprising swiftness. At first, every few steps were punctuated by, *"¡Aiiii!"*, but soon he learned to expect the trees to move.

Yaso caught on faster and, about a third of the way down, she took the lead. Genjo recklessly increased his speed. Alex felt a wave of panic. I can't lose, he thought.

"YOW!" Genjo cried out, as his shoulder clipped a tree trunk. He spun out of control, tripped over his own feet and skidded along the gritty sand straight into another tree, head first.

"Runner go down!" Kapua yelled.

Steadily Alex gained on Yaso. As he passed her, he heard the distant sound of Kapua wailing. "Genjo, wake up! Genjo, wake up!"

Alex wavered. *Forget the others. Remember the crystal balls. Stay focused!* said his mind. *Winning will not take away the shame of leaving a brother in pain,* said his heart.

"Arrrrgghh!" Alex screamed. He stopped.

"Yo! Alex!" Canila yelled. "The race not done!"

Alex charged out of the woods onto the swath separating his track from Genjo's.

"Runner disqualified!" Morph Al bawled.

Alex ignored him.

"Healing not work," Kapua wailed, when he dropped to his knees beside Genjo. "Don't know why."

Quickly, Alex laid his hands on the large bump on Genjo's head and began to hum. From far away came the yells of victory. After what seemed like eternity, the bump on Genjo's head went down like a deflated balloon. Genjo's eyes fluttered open.

"Nineteen seconds."

Startled, Alex looked around to find Morph Al beaming down at him.

He and Kapua helped Genjo to his feet. When they walked out onto the swath, a cheer went up.

Yaso ran back up the hill to meet them. Her face glowed. Alex's regret at losing vanished.

"You won!" he cheered, throwing his arm around her shoulders and giving her a squeeze. "I'm proud of *you*, honourable younger sister!"

Nirvana beamed at Morph Al when he popped up beside him. "I did a good number on him, but he still passed the test of the heart. We've found him."

"You still have to get him safely to the Guardians," Morph Al reminded him soberly, "and he must go freely."

THE LEGEND

THE GROUND BENEATH THEIR FEET BEGAN TO VIBRATE. At the foot of the hill, sand funnelled up into the air. The tip of a structure poked its way out of the sand. It rose steadily upwards, until it stood three stories high, radiating a strange and powerful force.

"What is it? It looks like a big amethyst crystal!" Alex gasped.

"It's— it's a rocket!" Yaso stuttered.

"It's our CLT, our Crystal Lightwave Transit. It can take you to the stars, or just around the corner," said Nirvana. "The time has come for us to move on."

After saying their goodbyes, they were met at the door of the CLT by a fierce looking black swan, bigger than any they had seen so far, yet when he spoke, his voice was mellow and gentle.

"Creetinks," he said amiably, "we are expectink you."

"Greetings," they replied.

"Folks, this is Tian, our faithful caretaker of the Crystal Lightwave Transit." As Alex and Yaso stepped into the building, Nirvana whispered out of the side of his mouth to Tian, "He is the one."

"Ze Link! Found at last! Aaah, ze universe be praised!" Tian whispered back.

Alex spun around to face Nirvana. "I'm tired of you people whispering about Links and stuff as if I can't hear. What are you planning behind my back?"

"Stars above, he knows nothink about ze legend!" Tian gasped. "Why did you not tell him?"

"He was not ready to hear."

"Well, I'm ready now," said Alex impatiently.

"Okay. Tian, will you do the honours?"

"Of course. Please to follow me."

They were in a massive chamber. Everything was made of crystal. Light streamed through the walls, casting rainbows everywhere. In the centre stood a circular pyramid seven tiers high. From the very top came the sound of gurgling water, and on each level, pads nestled in crystal gardens.

"What are those?" asked Yaso.

"Ze launchink pads."

Tian pressed a button on a railing with his beak and the floor turned into a moving walkway. As they circled the pyramid, Alex noticed that the triangular alcoves in the outer walls of the chamber were set evenly apart and that each was lit differently. They stopped at one with indigo lighting.

Alex and Yaso stepped into the alcove ahead of Tian and Nirvana. The air was much cooler in there.

"I smell a picture coming," said Yaso happily.

A misty face appeared before them and began to speak.

"Chief of the Waspachu, Grandfather Waiputu, was a wise leader," intoned a male voice. "He taught his people the art of illusion, and over time they became known as the Invisible People. Other tribes held them in awe, and for many moons the Waspachu prospered. One day, Grandfather Waiputu was fishing alone on the river near the Great Falls when a swan appeared. It swam gracefully towards him and when its webbed feet touched land, it turned into a child."

As the male voice spoke, holographic images began to appear. Alex and Yaso watched in fascination as the swan turned into a pretty girl just around their age. Light radiated from her as she touched the forehead of the old chief. He fell into a trance.

"She showed him the world to come," the voice continued. "He saw the coming of the fire-stick. He saw the tribes of the world fighting over it, for it gave them the illusion of great power. He saw them cease to care for each other and the gift of life. He saw rivers bleed and trees turn to sticks of chalk. He saw his people dwindle to a few. When the great chief came out of his trance, he returned to his benab in the forest, and although it brought great shame upon a grown man, he wept. He no longer ate and words ceased to flow from his lips."

"He gon die," Yaso whispered tearfully, as she watched the pictures flow.

"On the twenty-eighth day, he was so weak, his sons took him back to the riverbank where he used to fish, to breathe his last breath. There, the child-swan appeared to him again. 'Because you care so much,' she told him, 'the tribes of Earth will have one more chance.' She touched his forehead, and once again he became entranced. She took him to the beginning of the fifth cycle of the Celestial Flock of Swans, and he saw children like the child-swan being born all over the world; children with great powers, who could touch others with love and restore their faith in life. At the end, the child-swan cautioned, 'Be sure to awaken them when the Eel opens the way.' She passed on secret knowledge, then handed him a sacred bowl of flames.

"This time, the chief returned home with tears of joy. He gathered seven of his wisest elders and said, 'From now on, you will be the Guardians of Light, keepers of the sacred bowl of flames and the secret knowledge of the child-swan. The responsibility will be yours to see that the wisdom is passed from generation to generation, until the time comes. Let future Guardians of Light be chosen from all the tribes of the Earth.' So began the Legend of the Swan Children."

The hologram dissolved.

Alex and Yaso gazed at each other, overwhelmed. They knew that they were the Swan Children the legend spoke about.

Alex turned to Nirvana and Tian. "I didn't hear anything about a Link," he said tentatively.

"When the fifth cycle of the Celestial Flock of Swans began, the present Guardians gathered in a secret spot in South America to usher in the births of the Swan Children – your births – and to prepare for the Awakening," Nirvana explained. "As keepers of the secret knowledge, they knew that without a Link between the cosmos and Earth, the Awakening could not take place. Only a Swan Child who had received the sixth power could be that Link. Somehow, the information leaked out and the Agoutis appeared on the scene, kidnapping Swan Children. They've been looking for those with five powers just in case one of them received the sixth."

"Good thing I only have three," said Yaso, relieved.

"We think the Order of the Red Yowri is behind them."

"Who are they?"

"A secret society dedicated to destroying everything we stand for, but they could not stop you from making your way to us, Alex Springfeather. Now that you know, you must freely choose to be the Link. It's nothing you can't handle. Will you accept the role?"

"When is the ceremony?"

"Tonight."

"*Tonight*? But I have to find my panman."

"There may not be enough time to do both," said Nirvana ruefully. "You have to choose between the panman and your mission, Alex Springfeather, and you have to chose now. We will honour whatever decision you make."

The blood drained from Alex's face.

"Is not fair!" Yaso protested. "He has to get the panman, to find the feather and the fox, and Tia Lucia!"

"The world needs him."

"This is too much." Alex turned and walked away.

"Let him be," said Nirvana, when Yaso tried to follow. "The decision is his alone."

As Alex passed the green alcove, he stopped. A pleasing energy radiated from it. He walked in. The moment he sat down, the alcove disappeared and he found himself sitting under a jamoon tree beside a stream. He leaned back against the tree. He didn't feel like thinking. He just wanted to listen to the kiskadees calling to one another from the tree branches.

When he came out, Yaso and Nirvana were on the second tier of the pyramid, each standing beside a launching pad. Tian was waiting below.

Alex took his place beside Yaso. "My wisdom voice said find the panman, so that's what I'm going to do," he said determinedly.

"Good decision," said Yaso, patting him on the back gleefully.

"Well, the die is cast," said Nirvana. "Let's do it."

STAR PALACE

KLIPA, KLOP, KLIPA KLOP, KLIP, KLOP.

"Up! Up! They're coming!" Alex's eyes shot open. He sat up, surprised to find himself lying on the dusty curb. "You crash-landed. Sorry dude, forgot to teach you the finer points of CLT travel."

"The next time I go anywhere with you, I'm putting on a helmet."

"Blend!" Nirvana whispered urgently.

Alex slipped on his backpack and sucked in his energy. Seconds later, Ning-Ning came into sight, plodding steadily towards them. Ten Dolla was slumped over, fast asleep at the reins. Alex waited for the cart to pass, then hopped onto the back. Nirvana followed, immediately burrowing beneath the canvas covering the sacks of provisions and fruit. Ning-Ning tossed his head in mild protest at the extra load he was now forced to carry, but Ten Dolla did not stir.

Snuggling up next to Nirvana, Alex checked his watch. 00:35. It was working again.

"Do you think Yaso got home all right, Nirv?"

"The CLT never fails to deposit you in the time-space dimension you choose. Once you set your mind, sensors in the launching pads respond, plot the course, and bam! you're there. So what's the plan?"

"When Ten Dolla gets to the waterfront, I'll snatch his jute sack the moment his back is turned." Alex took out the bag of Stinking Toe from his pocket and dropped a piece on the road.

"Hmmm, something smells good." Nirvana rested his head between his paws with a sigh of contentment. Seconds later, he was fast asleep.

Alex forced himself to stay awake to drop the pieces of Stinking Toe for Yaso to follow, but eventually the rhythmic swaying of the cart lulled him to sleep as well.

"Ey! What you think you doin'? Put that down!"

The distant sound of Ten Dolla's angry voice jolted them awake. He was not on the cart. He had stopped for some reason and now he was hurrying back, grunting and swearing. The canvas sunk in as someone stepped on it. Alex heard the soft squishing of fruit being crushed. Ten Dolla brought his big stick down with a resounding CRASH! and the cart shuddered.

"HAW-EE-HAW-EE-HAW!" cried Ning-Ning.

"Fosker oats!" someone swore. The outer side of the cart rattled, there was a thud and *plonk, plonk, plink, plonk.* The person was off and running.

"ME BAG! THIEFMAN GOT IT! SOMEBODY STOP 'IM!"

"Nirv, did you hear that?"

"Let's go! Grab my tail!"

Up ahead, a drunken Ten Dolla gave chase, bobbing and weaving all over the road. Alex and Nirvana zipped past him at blinding speed. Stunned, Ten Dolla fell flat on his face with a yowl.

"Runner down!" Nirvana screeched to a halt. "You go on. Send an SOS thought if you need me."

"Thief from thief make the devil laugh!" a voice crowed in the distance. The shadowy form veered off the road.

Alex dropped another piece of Stinking Toe, braced himself and plunged into the darkness of a thickly wooded area. He soon picked up the trail of the thief. Running along a well-worn path, for a split second he was back in his dream, following the panman. The gap was closing between them. Around a bend, the forest gave way to a sloping field. Beyond the field, ablaze with lights, was a three-storied building, studded from top to bottom with golden stars. Each floor was smaller than the last, so that the building tapered upwards, ending with turrets on the roof. It looked like a castle. Astounded, Alex failed to see the leg blocking his path. He tripped and went slithering down the dewy slope.

"Oooohhhhhh!"

He looked over his shoulder. A girl of about fourteen was curled up on the ground. Beside her was Ten Dolla's jute sack.

"Look what you make happen," she moaned, clasping her ankle and rocking back and forth. "You break my ankle now for sure. Why you following me, eh?" she spat at him. "I din't do you nothing!" Her freckled face was smudged with dirt and twigs stuck out of her short copper curls.

Alex scrabbled back up the slope to her. The baggy calf-length trousers she wore were frayed everywhere and her legs were well scratched. He touched her swelling ankle. Angrily, she flicked his hand off, but he laid it on again and started to hum. Mesmerized, she watched him.

"Is it better?" asked Alex after a while.

"Fosker oats!" she breathed, wiggling her ankle freely. "You got the touch!"

She sounded nice enough, beneath the gruffness; not what Alex expected of a street thief.

"My name is Alex Springfeather."

"Mine was Quick Vic, 'til you ketch me." She grinned ruefully.

"See if you can stand up."

Quick Vic got to her feet and tested the ankle. "It like brand new!" she marvelled. "You know, I knew a girl from Golden Grove Road who had the touch. One day, some rough lookin' people came and take her. We never see her again."

Alex shuddered.

"They came for you too, eh? But you get 'way," said Quick Vic shrewdly.

Alex nodded grimly. He snatched up Ten Dolla's jute sack, untied the string around its neck and tossed the contents out.

"There you are!" he whispered, hugging the panman to his chest.

"Is yours? Boy, Ten Dolla hands really fast." Quick Vic touched the silver figurine admiringly. "You must be the reason I take the bag. So long I wanted to do it, but I never had the courage to thief from me father 'til now."

"Father?"

A shadow crossed Quick Vic's face. She stuffed Ten Dolla's belongings roughly back into the jute sack. "He left when I was small. Came back twice, but only to rob us. When mummy dead, he take everything but me. Ha!" she gloated. "Now he know what it feel like."

She marched towards the building and Alex followed her. Up close, it was even more spectacular. On the gold-railed balconies, palm trees swayed gently in the breeze, and on the roof railing, stone birds stood guard.

"What place is this, Quick Vic?"

"Star Palace. It uses to belong to the Friends of the Flame. Nice people, but they had money trouble and a rich man buy it. I never see him with no chil'ren nor no wife, but next thing you know, people start saying his chil'ren dead in a car crash, and the place haunted. Nobody don't live there. It supposed to be renovating, but I never see no carpenters, only people moving boxes. They come in full and go out empty."

"What's in the boxes?"

Quick Vic shrugged. "Even the guard, Henry, don't know. The rich man don't let nobody in his house proper, except people who like this with him." She wrapped her middle finger around her index finger.

"Hmm. Without the stars and lights, this looks a bit like a place I dreamed of. You're sure it's empty?"

Two shadows appeared at a third floor window and vanished. Alex glanced sharply at her.

"Is ghosts. Not a soul in there but them. Everybody 'fraid of Star Palace now, but not me. I wants to see a jumbie up close."

"Hello all. Everything settled?"

"Nirv, you made it!" said Alex happily. "Yes, I got it back. This is Quick Vic. Ten Dolla is her father, but he was nasty to her, so she stole his bag. Is he okay?"

"Up and running – in the wrong direction."

Quick Vic cupped a hand over her mouth. Her eyes were brimming with laughter. "Boy, it sound funny, you talking so sensible to a dog. Is just like the girl from Golden Grove."

"What's going on here?" came a commanding voice from behind.

They nearly jumped out of their skins. Towering over them was a heavyset guard with a very annoyed expression on his face.

Quick Vic breathed a sigh of relief. "Henry, I tell you already don't creep up on people like that."

"But you're rude!" exclaimed the guard. "How many times have I told you, girl, not to loiter around here? This is private property. All this land you see around here belongs to Mr. Barbero."

"I don't care. I not moving. The Friends of the Flame always let me stay."

Henry clapped a hand threateningly to his hip. "If you don't get your little hard-ears self out of here now, I'm going to shoot you, your friend *and* the dog!"

"Shoot, nuh?"

Just then, they heard the crunch of wheels on gravel. "I mean it, Quick Vic." Henry hurried to the front, neatly tying back his baby locks into a stubby ponytail as he went.

Unfazed, Quick Vic ran after him. "Why all the lights on?"

"Because I turned them on," Henry snapped.

"But that not usual. Something going on tonight?"

"Mind your own business." Henry trotted back to his guard hut beside the gate. A car was approaching, its headlights bobbing up and down along the long and uneven road.

Alex looked up at the third floor window again. "I wish I could see what's in there."

"You'll be able to see the roof, if you agree to be our Link."

Alex shot Nirvana a startled look. "What do you mean?"

"The Awakening Ceremony is gonna be here. With the help of Quick Vic, your panman led you right to it. Dude, I don't think we need any further proof that you are the Link. So whadya say?"

Alex's mouth opened and closed a few times in amazement, before "I accept," came out.

"Good."

"*Pssst!*" Quick Vic was standing with her back against the compound wall, beckoning frantically to them.

"I'm still going to try to get inside though," said Alex determinedly, as they ran to join her. "I have to see for myself who's up there."

Henry's voice gushed politely over the soft hum of an engine, as the limousine slowed at the gate. "Nobody here yet, Mr. Mento. You got what you wanted?"

"Yes, I got what I wanted," they heard a cool male voice reply.

"Every time that Mento man come, boxes moving," whispered Quick Vic excitedly.

The limousine disappeared inside the compound. Nirvana bounded after it and barely scraped through as the gate rumbled shut. A car door opened and closed with a muted click, then another.

"It's going to be a big night tonight. It's good the Guardians can still use Star Palace for the ceremony, even though it doesn't belong to the Friends of the Flame anymore. Mr. Barbero— "

"Cut the chitchat, Henry. Get the dolly from your backroom and meet us at the side door."

They heard the rattle of keys and the front door swung open with a gentle swish.

"Hurry, Saddles." The car trunk opened. "Get the other end."

Quick Vic's eyes gleamed. "Let's see what they doing."

They scurried to the driveway. Staying well hidden, they peered through the iron bars of the gate.

"They're carrying a long wooden box in," Alex whispered.

"Yeh," Quick Vic breathed, "and it look empty this time."

Once Saddles and Mento were inside, Alex tested the gate. It had an electronic lock.

"Well, come on. Don't let that stop you."

Nirvana sat calmly on the other side, daring him, but Alex stood transfixed, staring at the logo in the centre of the gate.

"It's the sign," he said excitedly, "the one squiggled beside Señora Lagrima's cane! Her killer may be here!"

Fingers trembling slightly, he touched the eel-like body with a swan's head on either end. In the centre was not a spiked ball, but a star with a bowl of flames engraved in it. Could this be the place his father said had the answer to many questions?

"That's the Star Palace sign. See? 'S' for Star." Quick Vic trailed her fingers over the design.

"I have to find a way in."

"Can't climb over. I try already."

Alex spied a keypad by the side of the gate. "I got it! Quick Vic, get ready to press the numbers on the key pad when I call them."

"Uh?"

"Go on." Alex covered his eyes, and 'saw' Henry putting in the numbers. "5 … 9 … 2 … 1 … 2, no, no, 3."

There was a sharp click and the gate rumbled open.

Quick Vic's jaw dropped. "Boy, you're a magician!"

Trying to quell the butterflies in his stomach, Alex marched in. As expected, there was no one in the front yard and the door of Star Palace was ajar. The limo was parked on the circular driveway just beyond the door.

"I'll go ahead and check around," said Nirvana. "Stay on the ground floor until I get back."

"Where your dog going?" asked Quick Vic.

"He'll be back. Just follow whatever I do."

They cut across the lawn and crept up the stone stairs to the gleaming purpleheart door with the golden knocker. Alex dropped another piece of Stinking Toe before they cautiously crept inside. The foyer alone was the size of a small house. There was scaffolding at the far end, but no other sign of renovations going on. Golden raincoat racks, elegantly carved mirrors and tables with lavish artificial flower arrangements adorned the hall. Glittering chandeliers hung like icicles from the high ceiling, reflecting off the enticingly sleek marble floor. The place looked grand, but the air was stifling in a very unpleasant sort of way. For a split second, Alex wanted to turn back.

Quick Vic, unfazed, ran forward and glided several yards along the floor with a giggle. Alex shook off his unease and ran several steps, skating right up to the entrance to the living room. His sharp ears caught the sound of voices and hammering somewhere

150

down the long corridor. He motioned to Quick Vic and ventured in. There was more scaffolding in the egg-shaped living room, which looked like a vehicle travelling through space. Portholes and stars had been painted on the midnight blue walls. Beneath the sheer glass floor, Earth and the planets revolved slowly around the sun. Rays of indigo and violet light streamed down from a cluster of twinkling stars in V formation.

"The Flock of Swans," Alex murmured. "Señora Lagrima showed me those stars through her telescope. I remember now."

"Fosker oats! Jumbies everywhere!" Quick Vic croaked, clutching at Alex. She was staring in fright at the dimly lit area across from the living room.

Alex jerked round and his heart stopped for a second. Twelve children stood in a shadowy circle, conversing with each other. A ghostly aura surrounded them and the bowl of flames each held in one hand.

"Ah ... hello," he said tentatively, moving closer. Not one of them responded. They seemed to be in a world of their own. He edged forward, half expecting them to turn into ghouls and spring at him, but they didn't. He reached out and tentatively tapped the shoulder of the one closest to him. "¡Aiiii!" he exclaimed, snatching back his hand and wringing it. In fright, Quick Vic scuttled back into the foyer. Alex ran after her, grinning from ear to ear. "Come back, silly, they're statues."

"Statues?" Scowling, Quick Vic marched up and touched one, then another. Lit from within, their intense resin eyes and flesh-coloured paint made the sculptures seem alive.

They walked around examining them curiously, until footsteps in the corridor sent them scurrying out of sight. Somewhere, a door opened. They heard a sneeze. Alex peeped. It was Nirvana coming across the living room.

"HENRY, THIS IS REALLY NONE OF YOUR BUSINESS," Mento's voice suddenly boomed.

Nirvana ducked behind the sofa and Alex drew back.

"I'M IN CHARGE OF SECURITY HERE," Henry shouted back angrily.

"AND I MANAGE MR. BARBERO'S CONCERNS. IN HIS ABSENCE, I'M THE BOSS. GO BACK TO YOUR POST *NOW*." A door slammed shut.

Alex peered around the wall. A man in a grey muscle shirt and black jacket came out of a passageway pushing a dolly. He was obviously Mento. He entered a room further down the corridor. After a while, another man came out of the room, pushing the long box on the dolly. He wore a colourful dashiki and had a dip in the crown of his head.

"Saddles ..." Mento's heels clicked along the corridor.

"Uh?" Saddles stopped beside the statues, just a breath away from Alex.

"When are those brain-dead lugs of yours coming? It's getting late."

"Soon come, suh."

"Those statues have to be on the roof before the Friends of the Flame get here to set things up. We don't want them snooping around. This house is off limits, except for the roof."

"I know, suh." A piece of paper was hanging from the side of the box. BJ Warehousing, Alex read, before Saddles yanked it off, screwed it up and stuffed it in his pocket. "What a thing, though, eh? To think stargazers can do hocus-pocus right here and make chil'ren all over the world wake up with powers next morning."

"It won't happen, so don't even think it!" hissed Mento, his nostrils flaring like a bloodhound's. "Are you on their side, or ours?"

"Ours, suh, ours! I just saying— "

"Well, watch what you say! Don't let them get into your head. Keep the hate flowing, the Rake said! They must not succeed! The world would be a dangerous place if any more power fell into the hands of children. Can't you see what's happening? Every day another parent becomes enslaved. Every year another company director says, 'Give them what they want.' *Governments* are listening to them! It's a conspiracy!" Mento was practically foaming at the mouth. "We have to grind them down," he punched his fist in his hand, "enslave them before they enslave us!"

"Man, the Rake really got you," said Saddles, taken aback. "Not because he had a miserable chilehood he gon confuse me brain. I ain't got nothing particular against chil'ren. I just doing this for the money."

"You're the worst kind!" Mento unclenched his fists and swung away. "By the way," he added, the pitch of his voice dropping abruptly, "Barbero's new title is Master Astrologer. Furthermore, he's one of the Masters of Ceremony for tonight. Don't make that idiot mad by calling him a stargazer. We have enough trouble with him as it is. Now get that thing to the dock and return pronto."

Saddles shuffled off and Mento returned to the back.

"That man should be in the Belview Asylum," said Quick Vic.

"Okay, I've got the lay of the place," said Nirvana, "Let's go."

Alex beckoned to Quick Vic and they dashed across to the living room. "Nirv, did you hear?"

"Every word. The race is on, but we have one up on them: *you*."

"How can you be so cool? We have to destroy them before they destroy us!"

"Bring it down, dude. Don't let the hate in this place get to you. It'll weaken your powers. We'll get them in our own time and in our own way. Now let's see what's in that third floor room. We'll use those stairs in the corner."

As they scuttled up a golden staircase, which spiralled into clouds painted on the ceiling, Quick Vic tapped Alex on his back. "What the dog say?"

"I'll tell you later."

On the third floor, they slid open the door to the corridor. It was empty except for two tables at either end.

"I can keep watch here," Quick Vic offered, her face still a little pale from the encounter with the statues.

"Good idea," Alex agreed.

Nirvana headed straight for the third room on the right. They listened. There was a faint hum of a machine. Alex tried the door. It was unlocked. Easing it open, he peered in. "Oh!" He recoiled automatically, pulling the door in.

"What was that?" Nirvana sniffed intently at the crack.

Alex peered in again, then flung the door wide open. "Not ghosts or real children," he said disappointedly.

Two life-sized cardboard cut-outs of children were attached to a toy train, which was whirring slowly around the room on a track.

"Well, well, well," said Nirvana, "someone has gone to great lengths to keep people away from Star Palace." There was a crash overhead and loud voices downstairs. "Saddles' buddies, I'll bet."

"Someone coming up!" Quick Vic hissed, poking her head in.

"There's another set of stairs at the other end of the hall!" said Nirvana.

They dashed down the hall and exited just in time. "Okay, we'll split up. I'll head for the roof. Maybe I can find out what mischief Mento is planning. Dude, make yourself scarce until the Guardians arrive."

"But something is not right about this house. I want to look around some more."

"Don't risk getting caught."

Put out, Alex turned and ran down the stairs two at a time. Quick Vic bounded after him. They made it to the side door undetected. As Alex turned the knob, he heard a metallic voice say, "Ground Floor," followed by a *ping*. They shot out just as the door of the elevator opened.

Outside, there were ixoras, ginger lilies, hibiscuses and buttercups planted on either side of the path leading to the front of the building. Concealed behind them, Alex and Quick Vic made their way cautiously forward. Near the front, they heard voices and crouched behind a tall ginger lily bush. Along came Mento with two people. Both had on workers clothing and wore caps pulled low over their faces. As they passed, the sleeve of the woman's shirt billowed in the breeze. Alex clapped a hand over his mouth to muffle the gasp that escaped his lips.

They waited until the trio disappeared indoors, then bolted. Miraculously, the front gate was open. They didn't stop running until they were well hidden behind the wall of the compound.

"They're here! At Star Palace!" Alex croaked, panting against the wall.

"Who?"

"The Agouti kidnappers!"

THE AGOUTIS STRIKE

HENRY LOOMED OVER THEM, HIS EYES BULGING WITH ANGER. "How did you get into Star Palace? Why were you dashing out as if ten jumbies after you? This is serious now, Quick Vic. Breaking and entering, stealing, that's criminal activity!" He dumped Ten Dolla's jute sack on the ground in front of her. "You dropped the evidence on the premises."

"We ain't steal nothing," protested Quick Vic hotly, "and we ain't had to break in. Alex use his power to open the gate."

"Shut up, Quick Vic!"

But she went on, her freckled face flushed. "We went to see the jumbies. That ain't no crime. Alex see Agoutis and he get frighten, that's why he look so. We din't do nothing else!"

"Agoutis? Power?" Henry peered into Alex's face. "What's your name, boy?"

"Alex." He jutted his jaw out defiantly. "We're not thieves."

"What did you say? Alex? As in Alejandro Vega Van Sertima, sometimes known as Alex Springfeather?"

Alex's mouth fell open. He nodded.

"And you saw Agoutis in there?"

Alex nodded again.

"Come with me." Henry gripped Alex's arm firmly.

"No!" Alex tried to pull away.

"Leave him alone," Quick Vic shouted, shoving Henry. "What if he see Agoutis? Agoutis all over the forest. Is a crime now to see a rat?"

"Be still!" Both Alex and Quick Vic stopped struggling at the tone in Henry's voice. Voices wafted down from the rooftop. Someone came to the edge and looked over in their direction. Henry pushed them up against the wall and waited. The person walked away. Henry knelt down. "Now listen, Alex, I'm on your side. I'm going to get you to safety. But first, tell me what you saw inside."

Alex rubbed his sore arm and glowered at him. "How do I know you're not going to throw me in jail, or something?"

Henry opened his shirt and showed him a pendant on a gold chain.

"The Mystic's Amulet!" Alex instinctively touched his own, which he kept under his T-shirt close to his heart.

"Now are you convinced? If I'm to help you, I must know what went on inside. Time's running out."

While Alex breathlessly recounted what he'd seen and heard, cars began to arrive. A short line had already formed along the roadside. People in indigo tunics were ambling up the driveway in groups, chatting and laughing. The limousine coughed to life and moments later, Saddles and Mento were seen driving away.

"They're off to pick up Barbero," said Henry. "They must have left the other two to keep an eye on things. Let's slip away now, while the Friends of the Flame are arriving."

"Where are you taking me?"

"The sooner you're in the Guardians' protection the better."

Minutes later, they were in Henry's compact car, weaving their way through Lower Awara at a spanking pace.

"That limo may be fancy but it can't take the small roads like my Suzie." Henry patted the dashboard fondly. "We'll get to the stelling long before them. Keep an eye out for that blue SUV, Quick Vic, just in case."

"How you know so much, Henry?" asked Quick Vic, craning her neck back to check. "I took you for a ordinary guard."

Henry smiled wryly. "My detective agency was hired by the Guardians to investigate the disappearance of young people like Alex. We've been on the trail of the Agoutis for some time now. It led us to Star Palace. Three weeks ago, I took the job as weekend guard, Friday, Saturday, Sunday. I've seen enough dodgy goings-on to know that we're on the right track." Henry glanced at Alex beside him. "What you've told me confirms everything we suspected. You know you're the only one on their list they couldn't kidnap. I don't know how you managed that."

Alex's head was in a whirl. "The panman helped me." He took the silver statuette out of his backpack and rubbed it gratefully.

"How?" Quick Vic took it from him and examined it again. "Fosker oats!" She almost dropped it. "It winked at me!"

Alex grinned, reaching back to take it from her. "It does that sometimes. Papi winks and Hamma plays a tune."

"Come again?"

By the time Alex finished telling her the story of the silver panman, they were at the waterfront.

Henry pulled up in front of a little roti shop at the end of Donkey Alley. "We're just a block away from the stelling."

He got out and scanned the area quickly. The street was deserted. The dockworkers, who usually parked their transport carts there, were long gone. A light streamed from the closed up beer garden opposite, spotlighting the car. Henry got back in and swung onto a grassy patch at the side of the shop. Well hidden, he shut off the engine and beckoned to Alex and Quick Vic to follow him.

A field of brambles separated them from the dock and its parking lot. *SKIBBIE STELLING* said the sign on the arch above the landing area. The parking lot was empty, except for a minibus and its driver, who was leaning against the bus waiting. *FRIENDS OF THE FLAME*, was painted on the side of the bus in big curly letters.

Henry took out a notebook from his breast pocket, and flipped it open. *Rare bird has landed*, he scribbled quickly. *Hawks around, three spotted*. He folded it and handed it to Quick Vic. "See that monument to

our Honourable Mr. Skibbie, the workers' hero?"
He indicated a statue surrounded by periwinkles in
front of the sign. "Try to get yourself there without
the busman noticing you. If he does, pretend you're
a beggar. When the Guardians disembark, hand the
bald one the note."

She started off.

"Wait." Henry rummaged around in the trunk of
his car and took out a raggedy long shirt and cap.
"Mento and Saddles have probably seen you knocking
about Star Palace. These would make a good
disguise."

When Quick Vic slipped off down the sandy trail
through the brambles, she really looked like a beggar.
While they waited, Alex wandered down the grassy
stretch. Beside the roti shop were three warehouses.
Alex looked up at the names. Chow Yee Farms, BJ
Warehousing, Patterson Trading Co …
BJ Warehousing!

Alex signalled to Henry frantically. "That was the
name on the box Saddles took out of Star Palace!"

Henry joined him. "Well, well. I wonder if he
brought it here? We should have a look." He stooped
down and examined the lock. "Very pick-able."

"You too fast for your own good, Henry. Hand over
the boy and I might let you go home to your wife,"
said a coarse voice behind them.

Swinging around, Alex's heart lurched sickeningly.
A wiry muscular man with a scarred face and a
boxer's nose was standing by the car with his arms
folded. His greasy curls were pulled back in a pony

tail and his gold tooth glinted ominously in the moonlight.

"It's him," said Alex hoarsely to Henry.

Henry drew his gun. "Don't come any closer, or I'll shoot," he warned. "Just back away slowly."

Suddenly the woman, who was crouching behind the car, stepped into the open. "Didn't your mummy tell you not to play with guns?" she scolded Henry.

With blinding speed, she hurtled a cricket ball at him. It hit Henry's hand with a loud PAK! sending the gun spinning into the brambles. Henry roared with pain and doubled over, holding his injured hand limply in the air.

"You broke his hand!" Alex screamed, putting his arm around Henry.

"Spinna strikes," said the man coolly, advancing towards them.

"Run, Alex, run!" Henry gasped through the pain. "Get on the bus with the Guardians!"

Alex looked into the hate-filled eyes of the Agoutis, and a blind fury swept over him. He wanted to smash their cruel faces. *Use your power, not your anger,* his wisdom voice urged. *Be the Swan Child that you are.* As suddenly as it came, the anger slipped away. Unclenching his fists, he turned away from them. Henry's hand was already beginning to look like a small balloon. Focusing on it, Alex began to hum. In less than thirty seconds, the bones began to knit, the skin lost its puffiness and Henry's hand was back to normal.

"What a cool cucumber," said the Agouti man in admiration. "Maybe we should keep this one for ourselves, Spinna, as an emergency doctor. Wha'ya say?"

"He not going to roll over like a puppy, y'know, Chopsy." Spinna sauntered towards her partner. "Coconut don't fall far from the tree. He gon be full of tricks like his mother."

Forgetting himself, Alex jumped up and rushed at her. "What did you do with her?" he yelled, hitting out wildly. "Where is she?"

"The Rake might tell you. Then again, he might not," she taunted. Laughing, Spinna sparred with him.

Henry suddenly lunged sideways and knocked Chopsy's legs from under him. Chopsy fell heavily and hit his head on the ground.

Spinna grabbed Alex and locked her arm around his neck. "Make another move, police boy, and you can say goodbye to your Swan Child," she snarled. She tightened her grip. Alex struggled briefly, then went limp.

Shaking his head clear, Chopsy staggered up from the ground. "You make a big mistake. BIG mistake!" He whipped out a cutlass from a hidden sheath in his pants. Peering through half-closed lids, Alex saw Chopsy twirl and twist the cutlass with awesome speed, shredding the front of Henry's shirt. "I am Chopsy The Cutlass King!" he roared. "You not gon forget this name after I split you in half like a watermelon." He raised his cutlass high in the air.

Alex came alive. He slammed his heel into Spinna's shin. With an agonized yelp, she let go.

"Silver Light, deflect his might!" Alex glowed like a light bulb and a blast of silvery light shot from him. It arched over Chopsy's head and dropped the moment he struck. Chopsy staggered backwards clutching at his own face and throat and gurgling.

"Yaaayeee! It worked!" said Alex, pumping his fists in the air, as he pranced towards Henry.

Spinna drew a cricket ball from a pouch on her hip and fired it at Alex's head. It hit and ricocheted off, heading straight back to her. The force was so great when it hit her stomach, she barely uttered a sound. She was propelled backwards and slammed against the wall of BJ Warehousing.

Alex jerked around as she crumbled to the ground. Amazed, he watched the glow around him fade. The light had protected him.

"Boy-o-boy, I'll never forget this day," said Henry, pushing himself off the ground.

Alex parted the shredded strips of his shirt. "Are you okay?"

"Just a couple nicks. I have to admit Chopsy is good. He could make good money on stage, instead of going around kidnapping people."

"Look! The Guardians are coming."

Henry looked through the tangle of bushes at the sleek, luminous white yacht gliding up to the stelling. It towered over the launches and canoes moored nearby. "About time. Look at Vic go. That girl would make a good undercover agent. She's gone right up to the limo to beg and they're shooing her off without a backward glance. She'll do it." He unhooked a pair of handcuffs from his belt. While snapping them on, he spied a set of keys on Chopsy's belt. "I believe one of these should fit." He tossed them to Alex. "I need to get another set of cuffs from the car for young Spinna here."

By the time Henry joined him, Alex was at the front of the musty warehouse trying to open the long box with a flat steel bar. Around him were crates of all sizes and shapes. Some had foreign addresses on them, others simply had numbers.

"Let me get that." Henry went around and carefully pried up the four corners. Handing the bar to Alex, he lifted the top off. "My God!"

The steel bar fell out of Alex's hand and clattered to the ground.

She looked radiant, like a bronze angel. Only her face was visible. Sheets had been packed around her body to keep it from moving.

"Who is she?" Alex whispered.

"I've never seen her before. What was she doing in Star Palace, and how did she die?"

"Hey, we back! We parked the minibus in Donkey Alley, so when the limo going back up with Mento and them others, they won't know we here."

Turning sharply, Alex saw Quick Vic coming towards them, beaming with success. She was accompanied by a tall man in a gold tunic. His wrinkled face glowed with a wonderful energy.

"I see two of the hawks have already been downed," he said jovially, his voice echoing across the warehouse.

Alex gaped. The voice was the same, but the person he left behind in Alma five weeks ago had an unforgettable mane of hair. This one had none at all.

"From the expression on your face, Alex Springfeather, I must conclude that my new look is somewhat less attractive than the old." The man's eyes danced with fun.

"Grandfather Talking Dove!" Alex was about to run to him when he heard a tiny sound coming from the box.

Henry, meanwhile, was hurrying towards the medicine man with his hand outstretched. "I'm glad to see you, man. We have a serious situation here."

"Wait! She's— she's opening her eyes!" Alex yelled. "She's not dead!"

Everyone crowded around as Alex pulled away the sheets bounded tightly around her. "Can you sit up?"

She looked around at the faces over her, moved her lips, but no sound came.

"Let's get her out of this stuffy place," said Grandfather Talking Dove, taking charge.

He lifted her up and took her outside. In the fresh air, she suddenly came to life.

"Help us! Please, help us!" she pleaded, gripping the medicine man's robe.

"It's okay, you're safe," said Grandfather Talking Dove soothingly. "Tell us how you came to be here."

"My name is Naiya, and I'm from a village in Central America." Her words tumbled out. "I was kidnapped from my home and brought to Star Palace in a box. There were others already there when they put me in the dungeon, and many came after me."

"Who else is in the room beside the Swan Children?" Alex broke in.

"A matron and a guard."

"What does the matron look like?"

"Tall and skinny, with short stringy hair."

Alex slumped back, disappointed.

"They put a special energy field around us," Naiya continued. "We could not use our powers to reach out to anyone, and no one could find us. The field made us angry and confused. Our powers were growing weaker by the day. I knew I had to do something. I had to make them think I was dead. I have never used my power to stop my breath and my heart for more than a few minutes, but I knew it was the only way to get out and get help, so I was determined to try. I prayed that someone would find me before they threw me in the creek or buried me."

"It was a dangerous risk to take, Naiya," said Henry, with deep concern. "What if Alex had not noticed the slip of paper with the name of the warehouse?"

"But he did," said Grandfather Talking Dove, "and we must be glad of that. You're a brave girl, Naiya. Now we must go into the lion's den and rescue the other lambs."

"I think Mento is the leader of the Agoutis," said Alex. "He hates children so much, it's–it's *increíble*!" He told the medicine man what he'd overheard.

"Sounds like the Rake might be the mastermind,"

Grandfather Talking Dove mused. "Who is this person, any idea, Henry?"

"No. Question is, how involved is Barbero? Is he a front? For a person who owns garment factories worldwide and has been honoured for the orphanages he built, Mento seems to think little of him. So what's our plan?"

"I'd like to find out who the Rake is, but the only thing that's really important is the ceremony. When they see Alex, they'll panic. They know the ceremony must start between 3:00 and 3:30 a.m. or all will be lost, so they'll try to stall. They don't know we know where the Swan Children are. Let's keep it that way for the time being and let the night unfold."

Grandfather Talking Dove walked over to Chopsy and Spinna. He delved deep into his pocket and pulled out a small box, which contained a fine netting. He tossed it at them. On touching their bodies, the netting expanded, turning into an army of red ants. Spinna and Chopsy wriggled and moaned as the ants spread out rapidly, scurrying towards their feet, arms and chest, nipping, until they both went limp and passed out. "When they wake up, they'll have a burning desire to confess. Henry, I suggest you lock them in the warehouse and come up with Quick Vic and Naiya. Keep Naiya hidden until I give the signal. Come, Alex, you will travel with us."

Grandfather Talking Dove strode off towards Donkey Alley. Alex grabbed his backpack from Henry's car and caught up with him.

"Why is all this happening, Grandfather Talking Dove? Why do these people want to stop the ceremony?"

"What we are about to do tonight will alter the way people see the world forever. Those who profit from other people's miseries want to keep things just as they are. Once the ceremony begins, though, they can do nothing to stop it, so we must hurry."

His head in a whirl, Alex picked up the pace. "But I don't understand. How did you come to be here?"

"A week ago, one of the Guardians of Light died and I was chosen to fill his place."

"Now you know the secret the child-swan gave to Grandfather Waiputu, right?"

Grandfather Talking Dove smiled. "I do. Soon you'll know it too, and much more."

They passed the Agoutis' blue SUV parked in the shadows and sadness descended on Alex again. "I was thinking … If Mami and I had come to stay with you in Cree Kee Forest instead of going to Corazon, she would be with us now."

Grandfather Talking Dove sighed. "If only we knew then what we know now. But you can't force destiny, you have to let it flow."

"Will you help me to find her after the ceremony? I know I'm close, I just know it."

"I'll do everything in my power." They were at the bus now. The medicine man turned to face him. "It took great courage to follow your wisdom voice through all the confusion and doubt. Because of you, the Legend of the Swan Children will come to pass.

Oji-kwe, Alex Springfeather, *oji-kwe hei!"* said Grandfather Talking Dove softly, praising Alex in Waspachu.

Bursting with pride, Alex climbed into the minibus to be greeted with cheers from everyone. Suddenly feeling very shy, he waved and quickly ducked into the vacant front seat. Grandfather Talking Dove signalled to the bus driver and sat down beside Alex. The driver reversed onto the main road, shifted gears and they began the slow journey up the hill back to Star Palace.

A man as huge as a sumo wrestler, sitting across the aisle, leaned towards them. "So," he boomed over the noise of the minibus, "our Link this?" Sweat trickled down his temples in rivulets.

"Yes, Segu, this is he," said Grandfather Talking Dove. "Alex, I would like you to meet Mr. Segu Malinka, Master Astrologer and Friend of the Flame. He is one of our Masters of Ceremony."

Alex reached beyond the medicine man to shake Segu Malinka's massive outstretched paw. In the seats behind, he glimpsed a sea of white hair. A mysterious energy enveloped him. Nothing could stop tonight's ceremony, of that he felt sure.

THE RAKE

Alex stepped out of the turret on the roof of Star Palace and came to an astonished standstill. In front of him was a stage ringed with bands of smoky light that rippled back and forth, changing colour constantly. In its centre stood a receptacle in the shape of a sleeping swan. The stage glowed softly like a moon, casting shadows over the intent faces of the twelve statues, which had been placed around its edge. Glistening balls tumbled out of the open mouths of the stone birds on the railings, turned to liquid and fell like enormous teardrops. The moment they hit the tiled floor, the drops vaporized into a pale, silvery-blue mist that spread across the roof. The mist had a sweet, tantalizing scent.

Inside the turret, the Guardians of Light were settling into the plush seats to wait for their channel, Sister Silver Spirit. Henry was at the gate and Quick Vic was with Naiya in Henry's backroom on the ground floor. Nirvana was nowhere to be seen.

Mento, who had ushered them up, brushed past Alex and strode towards Saddles, who was lolling against a telescope by the railing. He collared Saddles and dragged him out of earshot, or so he thought. Alex slipped back inside the turret and listened from there.

171

"Where are Chopsy and Spinna?" asked Mento roughly. "I told them to stay put. And that cock-and-bull story of Henry's about a sister taking ill. I don't believe it. When he, Chopsy and Spinna are absent from Star Palace at the same time, I smell a rat."

"No worries, suh. Chopsy them soon come back. They must be out making a last search for the Link."

"He's right in there, you fool, probably spying at us from behind the door! The Guardians found him before we did!"

"So this is our Link!" a voice suddenly boomed behind Alex.

He turned to see a stocky man bustling towards him from the direction of the elevator. His thinning brown hair was parted in the middle and slicked down. He looked vaguely familiar. *"Bienvenidos al Palacio de la Estrella*. I am your host, Señor Paul Barbero," he gushed, but his smile didn't reach his beady eyes.

Alex shook his outstretched hand. *"Mucho gusto,"* he muttered awkwardly.

"So you outstripped them all, eh? *¡Caramba!* You must be powerful – lucky for us." He tried to grin but it turned into a grimace. "One moment, *perdone me.*"

He swept through the doors and hastened to join Mento and Saddles, leaving behind a smell of dead flowers.

"The Rake is here!" he hissed to Mento, his voice filled with dread. "He wants to see you now!"

Mento drew in his breath sharply. "What did you tell him?"

"I said I had nothing to do with your failure. I did my part."

"You coward," said Mento, in a voice full of loathing. "You almost blew it numerous times, spewing out the wrong astrological claptrap, and I covered for you."

"That wasn't my fault, she—"

"Shut up! Come, Saddles, let's go. Paul, go to your guests and try not to behave like a blithering idiot."

Alex edged towards the elevator.

Grandfather Talking Dove had instructed him to stay close, but the medicine man was engrossed in conversation. "It's 2:15," he was saying to another Guardian. "The Channel, Sister Silver Spirit, should be here by 2:30. That gives us more than enough time to …"

Alex stepped inside and sucked in his energy. He watched his reflection disappear from the shiny elevator panels moments before Mento and Saddles strode in.

"You'll have to do what Chopsy and Spinna were supposed to do. Get it right," Mento ordered, as Saddles exited on the ground floor.

Mento stuck a card into a slot beneath the number panel and pressed a numberless button. Alex felt his energy expanding. Slowly but surely, his hands began to reappear. Mento stood in front of the door, nervously fiddling with a pen. My power is weakening, thought Alex, panicking. If he turns around …

The door slid open and Mento walked out without a backward glance, leaving the card in the slot. Alex heard someone approaching with an uneven gait. Boldly, he peeped. He saw a tall man with a stoop. He had on a red poncho. A straw hat cloaked his features. Alex caught a whiff of a vaguely familiar odour.

"Sir, we have everything under control," Mento started off.

"Don't lie to me," the man snarled. "You didn't get the Link. They have him."

"But I've set the backup plan in motion, sir. By the time they realize what's happening, it'll be too late."

"If you fail again, I'll have to kill the children." A tiny gasp escaped Alex's lips. "Is somebody there? Were you followed?"

"Not possible, sir, no. I came by elevator." Mento's voice wavered.

The Rake hurried forward to check. Alex jabbed the button marked "Top". The elevator door began to slide shut immediately. He breathed a sigh of relief. Suddenly, a bony hand slipped through the gap and stopped the door.

Energy, become small! Alex commanded hastily. He held his breath and hoped. As the door reopened, his mother's words came back to him. *You must never look in their direction. Listen with your inner being.*

The Rake stepped in and began to feel around suspiciously. Eyes downcast, Alex slipped out the elevator and tiptoed past Mento. Halfway down the hallway, he felt his energy expanding. He started running. His footsteps echoed down the hallway.

"There he is!" the Rake shouted. "We've got him!"

"Not yet," Alex muttered, as he zigzagged through the maze of murky corridors. He spied an exit door and ran towards it.

"Dude!" Surprised, Alex halted in mid-stride. There was Nirvana, hiding in an alcove behind an old observatory telescope.

The Rake and Mento were getting closer. Without a word, Alex continued on. He slammed the exit door hard behind him and dashed up the first flight of stairs loudly. Turning, he tiptoed back down and flattened himself against the wall.

The door crashed open just as he sucked in his energy. Mento ran up the stairs, breathing heavily. "The safety locks are on all the doors. He can't get out."

The Rake followed, moving swiftly. "Good!" he rasped. "We have him cornered."

Alex slipped back into the corridor. "Phew! That was close!" he gasped. "Nirv, how did you get here?"

Nirvana crawled out. "I heard Mento talking to someone, followed his voice and found a chink in the armour – a loose stone behind a rosebush. I climbed through the hole and there I was, a stone's throw from their secret dungeon. The Swan Children are in there and there's an energy field around them that stinks. I've been trying to break it down, but it's draining me."

"My powers are fading too! Where is it?"

"Straight up, to the left and then right. Follow me."

When Alex tried to approach the dungeon door, an overpowering smell of decay mixed with fear hit him. He almost gagged. "It's an invisible barrier!"

"Yup. It confirms what we suspected. Only a member of the Order of the Red Yowri could have done this," said Nirvana soberly.

"I saw an emblem of a yowri on the inside of the Rake's poncho when he came in the elevator!"

"Not surprising. We gotta move the Swan Children out now."

"But how?"

"Well, we can't go through the field. Only those of like energy can pass through unharmed. So we gotta destroy it. I'll power you up and you'll break it down."

"Me?"

Nirvana grinned at the shock on Alex's face. "Yeah you, Swan Child. Use your power. Look for the weak link. Yak, yak, yak! Link, get it?"

Alex rolled his eyes. "Yeah, I get it."

Steeling himself, he approached the field. He could feel the power of Nirvana boosting him as he closed his eyes and probed. He touched a spot and pulled back. *"¡Uf!"* he shuddered. Suddenly, he stepped to the side and stooped. He jabbed his finger at the air. There was a blinding flash and the force field vaporized.

Their yelps of victory caused a stir behind the door. "Who's there?" a woman's voice asked.

Alex felt around in his pocket for the keys that belonged to Chopsy. He tried the longest one. It worked. Slowly, he opened the door. *"¡Mira!"* he gasped.

Nirvana poked his head in. Lying on thin pads were rows and rows of children. Some moved restlessly, others just stared into space. Beside a table with a lamp sat the matron in a white smock and pants. She blinked at Alex and Nirvana, confused.

"We've come for the children," said Alex, walking in boldly.

A figure stepped from the shadows.

"Rico! I found you! *¡Bravo!*" Beside himself with excitement, Alex advanced. "Are you okay? Did they—"

There was an ominous click.

Alex halted, perplexed. "Wh-what are you doing with a gun?" The blood drained from his face. "*You? You* are the guard?"

The woman stood up, dropping her knitting. "Who is he, a friend of yours?" she asked roughly. "Mr. Mento never said anything about anyone coming for the children."

"I've never seen this intruder in my life." Rico's eyes were distant and lifeless, and his face haggard. "I must get rid of him. Nurse Beria, lock the door behind me."

"Wait!" Nurse Beria put a hand on his arm apprehensively. "You're not going to— No one said anything about—"

Rico shrugged her off. "I have my orders. Kill all intruders."

Alex gasped. "But Rico, it's me, *niño*, your sworn brother! Remember we were going to search for Tia Lucia and then we got separated?"

Rico began picking his way mechanically through the rows of children.

"Step back slowly, Alex," said Nirvana urgently. "The door is to the right of you. Don't risk your life. Once you're out, I'll take care of him."

Alex ignored Nirvana. "The police are coming, Rico," he said in desperation. "We caught the Agouti kidnappers and the rest will be caught soon too, so nothing will happen if you disobey the order!"

"What? Police coming?" screeched Nurse Beria, her eyes bulging with fear.

She made a dash for it, carelessly stepping on arms and legs in her haste. She slipped and lunged sideways, jamming Rico. His trigger finger jerked. BOOM!

Alex felt his body crash against concrete. Through blurry eyes, he saw an anguished look on Rico's face. The smoking gun slipped from his grasp and he fell to his knees. Nirvana dove for the gun, grabbed it with his teeth and sprinted out of reach. Alex heard the woman scream. Her footsteps receded down the corridor. He struggled to stay conscious. "I want to be eleven, I want to be eleven ..."

Something wet and cold roused him. Weakly, he opened his eyes. Nirvana was sniffing around his face.

"Welcome back," said the dog happily.

Alex struggled to rise. His chest felt as if an elephant had sat on it. "Rico shot me!"

He looked down. There was no blood, only a charred hole in his T-shirt. Bewildered, he felt around. His fingers touched the amulet. Grabbing the leather strap, he pulled it out. There was a dent in the middle of its dancing figure.

A flurry of footsteps sounded in the corridor.

"The children are this way!"

Alex got to his feet shakily. "What's going on?"

"I believe the Guardians are here."

The first to arrive was Grandmother Soroti, a stately Guardian, with two fat shoulder-length plaits of soft kinky white hair. "Are you okay, dear one?"

Alex nodded. "Rico shot me, but Grandfather Talking Dove's amulet saved me. How did you know we were here?"

"The moment we began to feel the presence of the Swan Children, we knew you had removed the energy field of which Naiya spoke," said the medicine man. "The time has come to end the drama which the Agoutis and Yowris began."

"Come," said Grandfather Khoi, the Guardian with a long, wispy white beard, "we must heal the Swan Children and take them upstairs. Time runs out."

A door slammed. Two pairs of footsteps tick-tacked along the concrete floor, coming their way.

"Mento and the Rake are coming back!" said Alex.

The Guardians closed ranks and blocked the corridor. Grandfather Talking Dove stuck his hand into the trousers of his tunic and pulled out a glass box with tiny holes in it. It was as big as the palm of his hand and in it, perched on a golden velvet cushion, were two dragonflies.

The two men charged around the corner and came to a stunned halt. At last Alex saw the face of the man they called the Rake.

"I know him! He's Rojo The Rake Thief from Alma!" he exclaimed in disbelief.

"Arrrgh!" growled the Rake in fury, raising an arm to shield his face. Spinning around, he vanished.

"Sir?"

Mento looked back. He was alone. The Guardians advanced as one. Mento turned and fled too. Grandfather Talking Dove released the dragonflies. A short while later, one returned.

"Well done," said Grandfather Talking Dove softly to the dragonfly.

They found Mento's body crumpled on the ground in one of the passageways, and the crushed body of the other dragonfly beside the old observatory telescope.

"I can't let Rojo get away," said Alex grimly. He dashed towards the elevator.

"Wait!" Grandfather Talking Dove cried. "It's too dangerous!"

Nirvana chased after Alex, barely squeezing through the elevator door. "What's got into you?"

"I have to make him tell me where Mami is."

The elevator opened on the ground floor and Alex dashed out the side door. At the front, he met Henry putting handcuffs on Barbero.

"The Rake got away!" Alex said breathlessly. "He's around somewhere."

"He's not going to get past me. I'll lock the gate." Henry yanked Barbero to his feet.

"Closing the barn door after the horse is gone,"

Barbero cackled. "He's already escaped." He eyed Henry slyly. "Let me go and I'll show you how he did it."

Henry snorted. "You'd do anything to save your own skin, eh? There's only one way out. We both know that."

"You're an arrogant fool, Henry," Barbero sneered. "For your information, there's a secret tunnel from the house, through the compound walls and under the ground. It leads to the woods."

Alex tore out of the compound with Nirvana, but they were too late. A flash of red, and the Rake's poncho disappeared into the darkness of the trees. Alex smashed his fist against the wall of the compound in frustration. Without a word, he retraced his steps.

A vehicle careened up the road and came to a screeching halt in the driveway, just as he and Nirvana rounded the corner to the front of the building.

"Alex! See him there? I tell you he not dead!"

"Yaso! Aunt Trixie, Uncle Fran!" Alex ran towards them.

"Are you okay? Are you hurt?" asked Trixie anxiously, getting out of the car.

Alex shook his head in a daze. "But— you're supposed to be in Moka!"

"I had a feeling something was wrong. Fran did too. He hopped in the plane, picked me up and we got back to find you gone, Sita in a state and Yaso babbling on about a Stinking Toe trail."

"It was a reckless thing to do, Alex, going after a man like Ten Dolla in the middle of the night," said Francis gruffly, coming around the car to hug him. "Thank God you're all right."

"You rescue the panman?" asked Yaso eagerly.

"Yes. But how did you find me by road, Yaso? I dropped the Stinking Toe in the woods!"

"It was easy," Yaso boasted. "I just—"

Talking Dove appeared, smiling. "Alex, it's time. Trixie, Francis, we meet again. And this must be Yaso. Come, we must hurry."

"What's going on?" asked Francis, utterly perplexed. "Alex never said anything about you being in Awara."

"We'll tell you on the way up."

THE AWAKENING

LOOKING SOMEWHAT FLUSTERED, Master of Ceremony Segu Malinka met them at the elevator. He had donned a downy brown and white striped poncho and was carrying a gong and a cluster of tiny bells. "At last, everyone here," he breathed, relieved. "Please guests to wait there." He pointed.

Quick Vic waved shyly. Beside her sat Rico, looking like his old self again. He shot Alex a look of mortification.

"We managed to undo the effects of the hypnosis," said Grandfather Talking Dove softly to Alex. "The police chief in Alma was the one who handed Rico over to the Agoutis. They tried to get information on you out of him, and when that failed, they brought him here as guard. He thinks you'll never forgive him."

Alex took the panman out of his backpack, marched over to Rico and handed it to him. "You take care of it during the ceremony. I want Papi to be here too."

Rico struggled with his emotions as he took Alex's treasured figurine. All he could do was nod.

"Come, Alex," the medicine man called.

Alex dragged Yaso along with him. "She only has three powers. Can she come too?"

"Of course! This event is for all Swan Children. Yaso, a special welcome to you." Grandfather Talking Dove bowed and Yaso looked fit to burst with pleasure.

"Channel came while you downstairs. We put her in room for quiet," said Segu Malinka as they stepped outside the turret. "We begin now?"

"Yes, Segu, we are ready at last." Grandfather Talking Dove signalled to Grandmother Soroti.

Grandmother Soroti clapped her hands. "Gather round, everyone," she called to the other Swan Children, who were enjoying their newfound freedom. "Before the ceremony begins, we would like to be sure everyone understands what the future will bring. The time has come for you to accept into your hearts and lives the wisdom you will need to fulfil your destinies."

"Indeed," said Grandfather Talking Dove. "Once you choose this path, there will be others like the Rake, Mento and Barbero who will try to bring you down. If anyone here would prefer not to receive the wisdom of the child-swan, you may say so now."

A round-faced boy with velvety skin and fiery eyes, stepped forward. "I am Kwame and I want to say we are not afraid."

"That's right," a sandy-haired girl chimed in, taking Kwame's hand. "I'm Carol and I know we're all ready to do what we were born to do." She turned to the others. "Right?" Everyone nodded eagerly.

"Good. We shall begin."

Malinka sounded the gong and tinkled the bells. The turret door opened and an imposing woman, tall and muscular, stepped out. She was swathed in a sea green sarong and held a blazing torch. Together, she and Malinka walked onto the stage and lit the bowls held by each of the statues.

"O Spirit of the Great Cosmos guide us on this momentous occasion," the woman intoned in a rich voice, placing the torch in the receptacle. "As Grand Master of Ceremony," she continued, in an imperial voice, "I, Tamana, call to order the gathering of the Seven Guardians of Light."

One by one, the Seven Guardians of Light took their places around the stage outside the band of smoky light. They all wore grey capes over their gold tunics.

"Swan Children, take your places on the stage." As they arranged themselves in front of the sculptures, Tamana added, "Our Link will stand at the head … good. Now we must take care of one matter before the awakening begins. It is not customary for outsiders to view our ceremonies, but our Link has asked for permission for his foster family and friends to witness the event. Some Guardians believe it is not wise, so you must vote. Indigo to allow, burgundy to deny. Guardian of Origins, Grandmother Soroti, please step into the Circle of Intent."

The stately Guardian turned her cloak inside out and stepped into the rings of smoky multicoloured light. A rash of shimmering blue spread through her cape.

"Guardian of Creativity, Grandfather Khoi …"

Grandfather Khoi did the same. His cape turned a sparkling burgundy. He shrugged apologetically.

One by one, Tamana called their names. Each time grey turned to burgundy, Alex grimaced.

"… and finally, Guardian of Expression, Grandmother Hull."

A short woman with ruddy cheeks and white hair that flowed to her waist flipped her cape awkwardly. There were three indigos and three burgundies. Hers was the deciding vote.

"Say yes!" Alex muttered under his breath.

She entered the ring. Nothing happened. A murmur rippled around the circle. "Oh, sorry!" she exclaimed. Quickly, she secured the clasp on the cape. A wave of shimmering blue rolled upwards.

Alex grinned from ear to ear.

"On behalf of the Guardians of Light," said Tamana promptly, "we welcome Francis and Trixie Chang, Rico Marquez, Henry Thomas and Victorine Fox."

Curious, Alex looked around. Quick Vic entered last and went to stand beside Nirvana. The hairs on the back of Alex's neck stood on end. In a daze, he watched Tamana step down. Malinka sounded the gong. The Guardians of Light focused intently on the stage and began to chant.

The turret door opened. There was a soft rustle of clothing. A waiflike woman, shrouded from head to toe in brown gauze, her face completely concealed, ran as lightly as a ballerina onto the stage. She danced and twirled gracefully around the receptacle, her clothing billowing behind her. A powerful energy began to radiate from the Guardians and flow into her. Her arms rippled like waves in the sea. Suddenly, the Channel stumbled. The chanting stopped immediately. A sound escaped the Channel's lips and with shudder, she collapsed.

Alex sprang forward.

"No!" yelled Tamana. "Do not touch her while she is still a holding vessel, her power can be devastating!"

But her warning came too late. Alex touched the Channel's arm. A bolt of electricity shot from her into him, knocking him backwards with such a force, he was thrown off the stage onto the ground. Winded and bruised, he lay sprawled, barely conscious.

Everyone was milling around asking questions, but Alex could not find the words to answer. A sea of faces swarmed in and out of his vision.

"Are you hurt? Can you stand?" someone was asking.

Alex struggled to rise. Grandmother Hull, who was kneeling beside him, helped him sit up.

"That's my mother, not Sister Silver Spirit," he mumbled, struggling out of the Guardian's arms.

A hush fell over the guests, but the Guardians did not seem unduly bothered.

"Hold still until I check you," said Grandmother Hull sternly. After she had probed him, she let him stand. "Don't make the same mistake twice," she added, when he made a move towards the stage again.

"You confused, Alex!" Yaso tugged him. "Is Sister Sliver Splirit– I mean, Slister Spiv– She's the Channel, not Tia Lucia!"

"No she's not! I solved the riddle, Yaso! Quick Vic is Victorine Fox! She's the fox and I am the feather!"

Alex stared hungrily at the motionless form on the stage. "It's Mami, I know it is."

"Well, Sister Silver Spirit it is not. Of that we are sure," said Grandfather Khoi. "We knew the moment she began to receive."

The Channel began to stir. Alex rushed to her. The others followed.

"Mami!"

She threw back her veil and scrambled to her feet. "Alejandro, *mi chiquito*, it really is you." She hugged him as if she would never let him go. "I dared not believe when you touched me."

"It took a long time, Mami," Alex whispered, "but I knew I'd find you in the end."

"I'm so sorry. What a fool I was! A man in the gadget shop told me my dear friend, Talking Dove, wanted to speak to me urgently."

Grandfather Talking Dove frowned. "But we agreed no go-betweens."

"*Lo sé, lo sé. No tengo excusa*. I thought we'd dodged those two, but there they were, in the restaurant next door, waiting to bundle me off. They needed an astrologer who was familiar with cosmic events. They attempted to kidnap Señora Lagrima, but she fled. Her heart gave out under the mango tree. So they took her telescope and other paraphernalia and came after me instead. All the calculations Barbero presented, marking this event, were mine. I tried to trick them one or two times, but when they threatened to break my limbs, I stopped."

"But if they wanted both of us, why didn't they

kidnap us together?" asked Alex, puzzled.

Tia Lucia smiled wryly. "Actually, they didn't particularly want you at first, except as free labour, because they didn't know yet about your powers. I fought like a tiger when Barbero told me they had put you in one of the Rake's orphanage sweatshops."

Alex gulped. "The Corazon Boys' Home! But I escaped."

"And that made them suspicious. They decided you couldn't be ordinary and started asking questions."

"They captured Maria for a while."

Tia Lucia's eyebrows shot up. "*Madre de dios*, poor Maria."

"So what happened next?" asked Alex impatiently.

"They imprisoned me in the home of a woman called Conya. She was supposed to impersonate Sister Silver Spirit. But Conya was careless tonight. She forgot to lock my door. I knocked her out and locked her in my room. By the time Saddles ambushed the Channel and brought her to Conya's home, I had already taken Conya's place. I wasn't going to let them destroy tonight if I could help it," added Tia Lucia spiritedly.

"Moon Woman," said Grandfather Talking Dove, taking his old friend's hand, "I must confess I was so centred on my task, I did not realize it was you until your son touched you. As my good friend Khoi said, we knew it was not Sister Silver Spirit, but since we sensed no ill will, we let you continue. Tell me, why did you stop channelling?"

"Guilt. This ceremony should not be tainted by deceit. I had to make myself known."

"Five minutes to go," Grandmother Soroti warned.

Drawing himself up regally, Alex offered his arm. "Moon Woman, will you dance for us now?"

With a look of surprise and respect, Tia Lucia took it. "With pleasure, Alex Springfeather."

In the days following the Ceremony of Awakening, newspapers around the world had their own versions of what transpired that night.

ALIEN INVASION: Extraterrestrials Descend on Beams of Light! the tabloids screamed.

SIGHTINGS OF FIREFLY SWARMS REPORTED WORLDWIDE! No Evidence Found to Support Claims, El Diario Internacional wrote.

DEADLY LIGHTNING STORM HITS S. AMERICAN TOWN. Chain Reaction of Electrical Activity Set Off Globally! Science Today reported.

ACCIDENT VICTIM AWAKES FROM COMA. Doctors Unable to Explain Spontaneous Healing! the Awara Chronicle headlined.

At the bottom of the fourteenth page of the Chronicle was a peculiar notice:

> RAKE TO CELESTIAL TEMPLE IMMEDIATELY. OPERATION SWANSONG IN PROGRESS.
>
> O.R.Y.

ACKNOWLEDGEMENTS

I would like to express my deepest gratitude to all who helped make this book possible, especially my husband, Roy Mendonca, whose support has been immeasurable, and my sister, Fay Marks, who often stretched herself to the limits to be my sounding board. Special thanks also to my brother, Michael Marks, for the Spanish element (any mistakes are mine), to my mother, Stella Marks, who taught me to reach beyond the stars, and to my sister, Marguerite Clayton, whose generosity of spirit knows no bounds. I am also deeply grateful to my soul sisters, Judith Lam and Jennifer Moe Wilson, for their undying faith in me, to my nephews and nieces, from whom the notion of Swan Children originally sprang, to Menaka Piyaratna and Phoebe Ogawa, who frankly and lovingly critiqued my first draft, and last but not least, to my editor Joanne Johnson, under whose expert direction the best in me was allowed to emerge.

www.swanislandhome.com

Island Fiction

Series Editor: Joanne Johnson

Look out for other fantastic reads in the Island Fiction series:

THE CHALICE PROJECT
Lisa Allen-Agostini

Ada and Evan thought they were two normal children, living with their father in Trinidad. But when they begin to look deeper into their father's scientific experiments, they discover secrets beyond anything they had ever imagined. Who is their unknown mother? What is the mysterious potion their father is hiding? And what is The Chalice Project?

ESCAPE FROM SILK COTTON FOREST
Francis C. Escayg

Under King Zar's sincere but timid rule, the Kingdom of Ierie is rife with corruption, on the brink of another war and in need of a true leader. Domino, a rebellious young Goan who seeks to avenge his mother's death, stumbles into the role of Hero only to find an even greater destiny awaits him in the Silk Cotton Forest.

NIGHT OF THE INDIGO
Michael Holgate

Marassa, a 15 year old Jamaican boy, is catapulted into a wondrous world of Natural Mysticism. His twin brother Wico is dying and no doctor on earth can save him. Guided by Kundo, the mystic warrior, Marassa transcends time and matter into an unknown dimension, a planet called Orunda. If he accepts his responsibility as a Marshal or "Warrior of Light" he can rescue his brother from the clutches of death. Can he over come all obstacles and prove that he is worthy of his title?

DELROY IN THE MAROG KINGDOM
Helen Williams

"If you look into River Mumma's eyes, something terrible going happen to you!" Too late, Delroy remembers his mother's warning. Is drowning his fate or is something worse in store? Becoming a marog is only the beginning. The king of these unusual frogs has chosen Delroy to succeed him, but first he must retrieve the king's magical stone from a venomous snake. Sloggingthrough underground caves and tunnels, faced with insurmountable obstacles, Delroy is tempted to give up and wonders whether he will ever return to his former life.

TIMESWIMMER
Gerald Hausman

Riding the seas with an ancient story-telling sea turtle named Odysseus, Luke journeys across the Caribbean and plunges into a remarkable adventure through space and time. Righting wrongs and saving lives, Luke and Odysseus encounter spiders that are men and lizards that are gods, all mixed together in a pepperpot stew of fantastic spice that blends fiery history with delectable fantasy.